Critical Approaches to *Welcome to Night Vale*

Jeffrey Andrew Weinstock
Editor

Critical Approaches to
Welcome to Night Vale

Podcasting between Weather and the Void

Editor
Jeffrey Andrew Weinstock
Department of English Language and Literature
Central Michigan University
Mount Pleasant, MI, USA

ISBN 978-3-319-93090-9   ISBN 978-3-319-93091-6   (eBook)
https://doi.org/10.1007/978-3-319-93091-6

Library of Congress Control Number: 2018952229

This Palgrave Pivot imprint is published by the registered company Springer Nature Switzerland AG
The registered company address is: Gewerbestrasse 11, 6330 Cham, Switzerland

CONTENTS

NOTES ON CONTRIBUTORS

Elliott Freeman is writing specialist and assistant professor at Jefferson College of Health Sciences in Roanoke, Virginia, USA. His poetry has been featured in journals such as *Blue Monday Review*, *Prick of the Spindle*, *Rust + Moth*, and *The Machinery*.

Grace Gist holds a Master of Science degree in Library and Information Science from Simmons College, USA, and is currently an assistant in the Center for Materials Research in Archaeology and Ethnology at the Massachusetts Institute of Technology, USA. She is also a Foley artist and sound designer with the Post-Meridian Radio Players in Massachusetts.

Danielle Hancock is a PhD candidate and associate tutor at the University of East Anglia, UK. She has publications available and forthcoming on the topics of the history and evolution of horror podcasting, national identity and horror radio.

Line Henriksen holds a PhD in Gender Studies from the Unit of Gender Studies at Linköping University, Sweden. She has published on the subjects of monsters, digital media, hauntology, and ethics in journals such as *Women & Performance* and *Somatechnics*.

Heidi Lyn is Associate Professor and Joan M. Sinnott Chair of Psychology at the University of South Alabama, USA, and has worked everywhere from Hawaii to Harderwijk in the Netherlands studying animal intelligence and communication, with previous positions at UCLA, the New York Aquarium, and St. Andrews University. She has published over

25 studies on the brain, cognition, and communication in chimpanzees, bonobos, and dolphins have been published, and she has also studied the behavior of belugas, sea otters, and walrus.

Andy McCumber is a PhD student in Sociology at the University of California, Santa Barbara, USA. His research lies at the intersection of environmental and cultural sociology, with a particular focus on topics such as the construction of place, cultural ideas of nature, and human-animal relations. He recently published a piece with Neil Dryden on digital narrative and place-making in Santa Barbara, California, in *Environmental Sociology* and another piece on aesthetics of nature in ecological crisis in *Nature + Culture*.

Dawn Stobbart holds a PhD from Lancaster University, UK, where she is an associate lecturer. Her articles on the presence of narrative in video games, graphic novels, have been published, and she has a forthcoming monograph titled *Horror and Videogames: From Amnesia to Zombies Run*.

Michael Patrick Vaughn is pursuing a PhD in the Sociology Department at Emory University, USA. Vaughn is also a certificate student in Women's, Gender, and Sexualities Studies. His research interests include sex and sexuality, collective memory, meaning-making and identity processes, HIV/AIDS, and mixed-method research.

Jeffrey Andrew Weinstock is Professor of English at Central Michigan University, USA, and associate editor for *The Journal of the Fantastic in the Arts*. He is author or editor of 20 books, the most recent of which are *The Cambridge Companion to the American Gothic*, *The Age of Lovecraft* (with Carl Sederholm), *Goth Music: From Sound to Subculture* (with Isabella van Elferen), and *Return to Twin Peaks: New Approaches to Materiality, Theory, and Genre on Television* (with Catherine Spooner). Visit him at JeffreyAndrewWeinstock.com

CHAPTER 1

Introduction: Between Weather and the Void—*Welcome to Night Vale*

Jeffrey Andrew Weinstock

Abstract In this introduction to the volume, editor Jeffrey Andrew Weinstock first offers an overview of the podcast's history and considers reference points and sources of inspiration for the program, before focusing attention on the program's juxtaposition of ordinary and strange, and the roles of voice and sound on the program. Attention is paid to how the program creates a sense of intimacy between announcer Cecil Baldwin and the listener, as well as to how the program subverts expectations. *Night Vale*'s humor and absurdity are also explored, as are the program's politics and values, including its anti-corporatism and emphasis on inclusivity.

Keywords Absurdity • Anti-corporatism • Diversity • History • Humor • Inclusivity • Influences • Intimacy • Music • Politics • Values

J. A. Weinstock (✉)
Department of English Language and Literature, Central Michigan University, Mount Pleasant, MI, USA
e-mail: jeffrey.weinstock@cmich.edu

J. A. Weinstock (ed.), *Critical Approaches to* Welcome to Night Vale,
https://doi.org/10.1007/978-3-319-93091-6_1

> *Lights, seen in the sky above the Arby's. Not the glowing sign of Arby's.*
> *Something higher and beyond that. We know the difference. We've*
> *caught on to their game. We understand the lights above the Arby's*
> *game. Invaders from another world. Ladies and gentlemen the future*
> *is here. And it's about a hundred feet above the Arby's. (Fink and*
> Cranor, Mostly Void 7)

As *Welcome to Night Vale* co-creator Joseph Fink tells it in the introduction to *Mostly Void, Partially Stars*, the published transcripts to the first 25 episodes of *Night Vale*, the paragraph above about lights above the Arby's—which appears in the pilot episode ("Pilot")—was the first bit written for the program and captured the "mood" he was hoping to achieve. "For a long time after," continues Fink, "when I was trying to make something fit the world of Night Vale, I thought back to that first paragraph I wrote and tried to capture the same feeling I had when I wrote it" (Fink, "Introduction" xviii). In starting to think critically about *Night Vale*—about what it is, what it means, how it means, why it has become so popular, why it matters, and so on—perhaps we can let ourselves be directed by Fink, who points out for us a particularly rich and resonant passage present from the start and highlights for us the roles of "mood" ("Introduction" xviii) and "feeling" in his own consideration of the program. So let us begin, like Fink, with two lights against the backdrop of the night sky. The first is the familiar red and white neon sign of the fast food chain (probably the one with the name plastered across the front of the outline of a cowboy hat)—real-world, working class (maybe even a bit red-necky) everyday American capitalism. And then we mentally pan up to the other light, "something higher and beyond that," the antithesis of the commonplace first. In the space of "about a hundred feet," we shift our view from the quotidian to the interstellar, from the familiar world of weather to the mysteries of the universe and the void—and we find them in close proximity, one literally hovering over the other. The sublime—extraterrestrial life and the profound expanse of the universe—comingling with the profane in a kind of cosmic comedy: aliens at the Arby's.

In intertwining the familiar with the weird and exotic, *Welcome to Night Vale*, for all its brilliant strangeness, participates in a well-established narrative tradition. In order, therefore, to consider what *Night Vale* does that is new, it is useful to cast a backward glance over its generic affinities. First, however, a bit of background on just what *Night Vale* is may be useful.

Typically airing on the 1st and 15th of each month, *Welcome to Night Vale* is a podcast—an episodic series of digital audio files that can be streamed online or downloaded. Premiering on June 15, 2012, the series purports to be a community radio program broadcast from the fictional town of Night Vale. Located somewhere in the Southwestern US, Night Vale is, as characterized by Fink, "a town where every conspiracy theory is true and people just have to go on with their lives" ("Introduction" xviii). Described variously as "'*A Prairie Home Companion*' with LSD in its drinking water" (Barton), a place "where David Lynch meets 'The Twilight Zone'" (Baker-Whitelaw), "like a local news Twin Peaks" (Virtue), and "Lake Wobegon meets H.P. Lovecraft" (Maksym), *Night Vale*, as co-creator Jeffrey Cranor explained in a National Public Radio interview, presents "a mundane, quaint American town, sort of overrun by ghosts, or spirits, or conspiracies or underground societies" ("Welcome to 'Night Vale'").

From humble beginnings in June of 2012 with 50 total downloads in its first week, the program's popularity swelled until in August of 2013, two months into its second year, *Night Vale* surpassed the podcasts *Radiolab* and *This American Life* to become the #1 podcast on iTunes, having been downloaded 8.5 million times in August alone (Cranor, "Introduction" xiv). Cranor attributes this success to fan enthusiasm on the social networking website Tumblr—and then correlates this enthusiasm with three factors: solid writing, originality, and perhaps most importantly, the program's representation of the same-sex relationship between Night Vale Public Radio (NVPR) host Cecil Palmer (voiced by Cecil Baldwin) and scientist Carlos (originally voiced by Jeffrey Cranor until episode 17, and then voiced by Dylan Marron). Max Sebela, a creative strategist at Tumblr, reported that fandom began to "spiral out of control" on Tumblr starting around July 5, 2013, with over 183,000 individual blogs and 680,000 *Night Vale*-related notes in a one-week period following episode 27, "First Date," in which Cecil recounts his first date with Carlos (Carlson). "Many fans have told us that this relationship means so much to them," writes Cranor (xv). As Bottomley observes, "the podcast has consistently remained in or near iTunes' Top 20 rankings in the United States ever since [August of 2013], and regularly charts internationally too" (179). The success of the podcast, which in December of 2016 celebrated its 100th episode, has subsequently led to several touring live *Night Vale* shows and two novels so far set in the *Night Vale* universe: *Welcome to Night Vale: A Novel* (2015) and *It Devours!* (2017).

For Bottomley, the success of *Night Vale*, "an independent production, made on a shoestring budget by a small group of creative personnel with no ties to the traditional radio industry, a podcasting network, or any other major media institution" (182), is all the more remarkable for its doing so "in a space increasingly dominated by professional media producers" (180). While celebrating *Night Vale*'s uniqueness, however, Bottomley does offer a helpful overview of how the program arrives at its unusual format through the "remediation"—the appropriation and refashioning—of older media forms: notably radio drama and community and talk radio. The podcast, as a scripted narrative written, performed, and produced to be heard, explains Bottomley, is a throwback to the days of radio drama (183), and *Night Vale*'s generic affinities—a mix of comedy, science fiction, and horror—recalls the most popular forms of programming during the "golden age" of radio during the 1940s and 1950s. *Welcome to Night Vale*, although a podcast, carries on the tradition of radio programs such as *Inner Sanctum Mystery* (1941–1952) and *The Mercury Theatre on the Air* (1938) (the latter of which is perhaps most famous for the broadcast of its adaptation of H.G. Wells' *The War of the Worlds* on October 30, 1938, and the ensuing panic). Bottomley also points out that, while the topics Cecil discusses on *Night Vale* may be unusual, his presentation of them is actually quite familiar, as its use of the primary codes of radio production—speech, music, noise, and silence—are in keeping with standard radio production (185). And while Cecil's quirky commentary or confessional moments may not correspond to the kind of news presentation one is used to from American National Public Radio, for example, there is nevertheless "a long and rich history of more marginal forms of talk radio" (186) from which *Night Vale* borrows. Radio practices familiar to us today from talk radio and community radio "provide the context in which [*Night Vale*'s] narrative operates as entertainment" (Bottomley 185).

Night Vale, too, as its creators acknowledge, derives inspiration from a range of literary, televisual, and cinematic sources, both older and contemporary. The horror fiction of H.P. Lovecraft is one frequent point of reference and seems especially apropos given that *Night Vale* co-creator Jeffrey Fink served as the editor for a 2010 anthology of fiction titled *A Commonplace Book of the Weird: The Untold Stories of H.P. Lovecraft*—a collection of weird fiction to which both he and Cranor contributed stories. Lovecraft's weird fiction of the 1920s and 1930s is built on the premise that the universe is a much stranger place than human beings acknowledge and that human achievement counts for very little when considered in light of deep time and immensely powerful alien races. Fink, it should be noted, has more recently come out against Lovecraft; in a 2013 interview with the online site Brainwashed, he stated that,

> This is going to put off some of our fans, but I actually hate Lovecraft, both personally and for his writing. I don't think anyone can deny that he was a shitty person. His whole "cosmic horror" thing mainly came out of his intense racism. And I think that, on a prose level, he was also a deeply shitty writer. I mean his stuff is almost unreadable for me.
>
> That said, I think he was brilliant on an idea level, and that's definitely where we connect with him. Our Lovecraft book, for me, is a way of leaving behind all vestiges of his writing, including the stupid names of his gods, while keeping the brilliance of his unnerving ideas and images.

Fink continues,

> *Night Vale* is often called Lovecraftian, but we never consciously chose to make it that way. I just think Lovecraft, awful writer that he was, has had such an impact on modern horror and science fiction that it's impossible to work in that field without using some of the ideas he generated. Which kind of annoys me, but I respect the old racist bastard all the same. (D'Amico)

Despite Fink's reservations however, Lovecraft's influence arguably pervades *Night Vale* and can perhaps be seen most clearly in *Night Vale*'s representations of dimensional rifts and powerful entities such as the Distant Prince, Huntokar, the demonic beagle puppy, and so on that intrude upon the town's existence—as well as in the weirdness of Night Vale more generally.

Other obvious reference points and sources of inspiration include *The Twilight Zone*, *The X-Files*, and the works of David Lynch—most especially the original run of *Twin Peaks*. *The Twilight Zone* series, which originally ran from 1959 to 1964 and then was revived twice (1985–1989 and then again 2002–2003), itself drew inspiration from earlier television and radio programs making use of science fiction and fantasy tropes as it offered compact narratives of parallel universes, apocalyptic scenarios, extraterrestrials, and supernatural creatures. Some narratives staged intrusions of foreign entitles and elements into a world recognizably our own; others immersed viewers in an exotic other worlds. Framed in the original run by creator Rod Serling's commentary (which resonates with Cecil's own opening and concluding commentary to teach *Night Vale* episode), episodes were stand-alone and primarily plot driven.

The American science fiction television series *The X-Files*, which aired from 1993 to 2002, is another important link in the chain of influences when considering *Welcome to Night Vale*. Created by Chris Carter, this series focused on two FBI investigators—Fox Mulder (David Duchovny) and Dana Scully (Gillian Anderson)—called upon to investigate so-called X-Files: mysterious unsolved cases. In addition to the "monster of the week" episodes in which Mulder and Scully explored seemingly paranormal occurrences, monsters, and the like, the series also developed a larger on-going story arc involving a government conspiracy to hide the existence of and human interaction with extraterrestrials. Some episodes also introduced a comic tone. *Night Vale* has inherited from *The X-Files* its post-Watergate conspiracy theory insistence, as well as its preoccupation with alien forces and things that go bump in the night.

While any overview of *Night Vale*'s origins needs to take into consideration *The Twilight Zone* and *The X-Files*, an even more important reference point is arguably the original run of the TV series *Twin Peaks*, and the works of director David Lynch more broadly. Like *Welcome to Night Vale*, *Twin Peaks* introduced us to a community of quirky characters and a town that is both a part of the world we know, while simultaneously set apart from it. (In this, *Twin Peaks* drew inspiration from other narratives featuring small towns populated by grotesque and/or supernatural characters, such as Sherwood Anderson's 1919 *Winesburg, Ohio* and the long-running TV serial *Dark Shadows* [original run 1966–1971], which featured the vampire Barnabas Collins, together with other supernatural creatures.) As FBI special agent Dale Cooper (Kyle McLachlan) investigates murder in Twin Peaks, he interacts with characters such as The Log Lady (Margaret Coulson) who seemingly receives messages from a log she carries; has encounters with the spirit world including a giant (Carl Struycken), a red-suited little person (The Man from Another Place, played by Michael J. Anderson), and the demon BOB (Frank Silva); and ultimately at the end of the initial run enters another realm (the dreaded Black Lodge). From *Twin Peaks*, *Night Vale* inherited the strategy of mixing the comic with the dark, of foregrounding both diegetic and non-diegetic music, and of introducing listeners to a world pervaded by weirdness. *Night Vale*'s indebtedness to *Twin Peaks* is perhaps signaled by the name of NVPR announcer Cecil *Palmer*—a surname he shares with the murdered girl in *Twin Peaks*, Laura Palmer (Sheryl Lee), and her father Leland (Ray Wise) who turns out to play a crucial role in the series. Beyond *Twin Peaks*, the other works of director David Lynch could be added into the mix of influences as well.

As in *Twin Peaks*, Lynch characteristically infuses his films with a sense of the weird lurking just beneath the façade of normalcy as quirky characters encounter strange (and sometimes paranormal) occurrences—all of which seems very apropos of *Night Vale*.

Although Lovecraft, *The Twilight Zone*, *The X-Files*, and David Lynch all are relevant points of comparison and sources of inspiration for *Night Vale*, Fink and Cranor themselves have also identified a number of perhaps less expected influences. In an interview with Lindsey Weber for the online zine *Vulture: Devouring Culture*, the two referenced not only Stephen King and Lynch's *Twin Peaks: Fire Walk With Me*, but author Thomas Pynchon, Sports Talk Radio, and the band The Mountain Goats (Weber). *Welcome to Night Vale* itself often references works of literature, most frequently in connection with character Tamika Flynn (voiced by Symphony Sanders), whose reading has apparently included Alan Paton's *Cry, the Beloved Country*, Willa Cather's *Death Comes for the Archbishop*, Italo Calvino's *Invisible Cities*, Bertolt Brecht's play *Life of Galileo*, John Osborne's play *Look Back in Anger*, Emily Dickinson's poetry, and Milorad Pavic's *Dictionary of the Khazars*. Despite Cecil's protestations that reading books "makes us deviants, perverts, freaks" and that "books are dangerous and should be avoided" (episode 76, "An Epilogue"), *Night Vale* as a series clearly celebrates on both explicit and implicit levels literary culture—indeed, the show includes among its target audience what Cecil calls "book reading freak[s]" (episode 76).

What this consideration of sources of inspiration and generic affinities suggests is that *Welcome to Night Vale*, unique as it may be, did not emerge *ex nihilo*; rather, the program instead participates in various literary, media, and cultural traditions as it appropriates and refashions older forms, and draws inspiration from other works. This is of course true of any cultural artifact—it is not meant as a slight against *Night Vale*, nor does it undercut the originality or success of the program. Instead, appreciating what is familiar in *Night Vale* allows us then to consider more clearly what it is doing that is new and different. With that in mind, let's return to our beginning and the lights above the Arby's from the pilot episode.

For Fink, the lights of the Arby's passage represents the mood he was trying to create, and I think it is fair to say that the passage does indeed capture much of the essence of *Welcome to Night Vale*, a podcast that consistently mingles the common and the strange. Like extraterrestrial lights above the Arby's, *Night Vale* repeatedly mixes the everyday with the extraordinary, offering us a floating cat in a men's room or angels (if angels exist—a subject of some debate on the program for quite a while) changing light bulbs or a tiny city beneath lane five of a bowling alley or a ghost coaching a Little League team. The "beyond" the Arby's, we realize, is not really beyond us at all, not somewhere out there, but rather above, below, and all around us, and the universe as a consequence is a much stranger—and more dangerous, and often far funnier—place than we ever imagined.

In addition to juxtaposing the ordinary and the extraordinary, however, there are two other essential elements to the lights above the Arby's passage that speak to the overall mood and feeling of *Night Vale*. The first we can put our finger on in a relatively straightforward way—and that is the "we." "*We* know the difference. *We've* caught on to their game. *We* understand the lights above the Arby's game." This is not *The X-File* or *Twin Peaks* or any other program in which mysterious and supernatural events take place eliciting dismay and amazement from both characters and viewers. As Mike Rugnetta points out in his excellent video blog segment on *Night Vale*, a crucial difference between Lovecraftian horror (or, for that matter, *X-Files* horror or even that of *Twin Peaks*) is that in *Night Vale*, Lovecraft's "paralytic terror" is replaced with into "drab mundanity" (Rugnetta). That is, rather than the revelation of cosmic forces driving protagonists insane, the weird is the norm in *Night Vale* and "we" are eavesdropping on a program intended for Night Vale insiders in the know. NVPR announcer Cecil and his listeners take for granted the existence of five-headed dragons and forbidden dog parks and houses that appear to be there but aren't. They—and to the extent that we ourselves are interpolated into the program as NVPR listeners, "we"—know not only the game of the lights in the sky above the Arby's but all about the sheriff's secret police and the strange habits of the town council and about a vague but menacing government agency. NVPR listeners are familiar with the perils of street cleaning day and fashion week and librarians. Cecil assumes that "we" not only know the details and people of Night Vale (although we may need a little reminding about John Peters, you know), but that we participate in what we could refer to as Night Vale's "structure of feeling," the unstated assumptions shared by those living there about how the world works, including, as will be discussed next in more depth, an easy acceptance of diversity. Part of the feeling of *Night Vale*, therefore, is the sense that we are overhearing a broadcast from a different world—one that in many respects works according to a different logic. We haven't gone through the looking glass exactly; rather, we're listening to a magic radio that broadcasts to us messages from a parallel universe (that itself at times has its own parallel universes).

The second element of *Night Vale*'s "feeling" is harder to pin down because it has to do not with what the text means, but how it is conveyed—that is, with aesthetics and performance. Consider again the lights above the Arby's passage and note the sequence of short, declarative phrases built around the repetition of keywords: lights, Arby's, we, above. There is poetry here in the long vowel sounds, the sibilance of "lights seen in the sky above the Arby's," the haiku-like precision, the concise narrative beginning and ending with "above the Arby's." As Elliott Freeman develops in his contribution to this collection, *Welcome to Night Vale* often revels in the aesthetic qualities of language—the sensuous of words, how they feel in the mouth and flow together. Just consider, for example, episode 61, built around the repetition of the phrase "Briny Depths" ("Briny Depths") or the intoning of "Hulu" during the "message from our sponsors" segment of episode 42 ("Numbers"), or Cecil's increasingly exaggerated "Who's a good boy?" in episode 91, "Who's a Good Boy?" Part of the mood and feel of *Night Vale* has to do with the sound of words and phrases. On one level indeed, *Night Vale* is all about language—not only its abilities to convey both meaning and feeling, but the way its material qualities facilitate, amplify, or diminish its abilities to serve as a conduit for meaning.

Now, add in what may be as central to *Night Vale*'s success as the writing: "the voice of Night Vale," as Cecil Baldwin who performs Cecil Palmer is referred to in the credits at the end of each program. If you are a fan of *Night Vale*, then, when you read the epigraph at the start about the lights above the Arby's, you likely "heard" it in your head as spoken by Cecil (and, if you didn't before, you will now!). It wasn't until the 16th episode of *Night Vale* ("The Phone Call") that a voice other than Cecil's was introduced into the program and, even after over 100 episodes, Cecil's remains the primary voice. *Welcome to Night Vale* is therefore inextricably interconnected with Cecil's voice; indeed, *Welcome to Night Vale* is arguably all about "the voice of Night Vale," both in the sense that it is focused on Cecil—his life, relationships, thoughts, preferences, and so on—and in the sense that it is about his voice and delivery. As performed by Cecil, the lights above the Arby's passage comes across as part love poem, part lullaby: soothing, measured, and precise—the melancholic feel of Cecil's rich timbre then accentuated by what seems to be a non-diegetic music bed consisting of spacey electronics; romantic, deeply reverbed piano; and machinic noises that echoes Cecil's "*above* the Arby's" by rising slowly in steps into the next segment until it then starts to descend in a slow arpeggio. Like poetry, *Night Vale* is often as much for the ear as for the mind, and its delivery—Cecil Baldwin's performance, together with other voices, silence, and both diegetic and non-diegetic music and sounds—is a crucial component in creating its effect.

Music, it should be mentioned, plays a particularly important role in the program. Deviating a bit from the conventions of talk radio, many of Cecil's segments are voiced overtop a music bed that helps to create a particular mood. There is no sense that Cecil is selecting the music himself, and this would seem to be an example of postproduction effects being added. While seldom overly intrusive, the music beds do add a curious tension to the "community radio" format that at once makes the program seem more professional and less "real." Music also plays an equally curious and even more explicit role in the form of the musical performances that are presented as "the weather." At some point in each episode of *Night Vale*, Cecil pauses for the weather and a seemingly random song is played. Genre varies from episode to episode. (Fink mentions in *Mostly Void* that, when asked how this convention of the series came about, he has to answer that he just doesn't know: "Like a lot of my creative decisions … I don't have any sort of rational account of my reasoning. It just felt right and I went with it" [1].)

A close consideration of the "lights above the Arby's" passage in terms of themes, aesthetics, and delivery is therefore productive because it helps us focus in on strategies the program uses to create its characteristic feel and engage listeners, which arguably cluster around the idea of proximity—understood both literally and figuratively. First, we can think in terms of literal proximity—position in space. While we don't know precisely where the town of Night Vale is, nevertheless, the community radio show format with Cecil as announcer addressing Night Vale residents establishes a sense of intimacy and immediacy. Cecil is speaking directly *to us*—indeed, episode 13, "A Story About You," is presented using the second person—and Cecil's nearness to the microphone and the general absence of special effects such as reverb create the illusion of *nearness*. Not only is he addressing the ladies and gentlemen of Night Vale, which may include us if we like, but if we close our eyes, we can easily imagine that Cecil is *physically* present with us, talking directly to us. This sense of presence may be accentuated by podcast listening practices that, unlike earlier radio programs of the 1940s and 1950s, often include headphones.

This sense of intimacy is further accentuated by the personal details and opinions that Cecil includes in his broadcasts, such as about his attraction to Carlos and his epic dislike for his brother-in-law Steve Carlsberg. As

Grace Gist discusses in this collection, our close proximity to Cecil—both in the literal sense of physical presence and the metaphorical sense of intimacy of relation—participates in constructing a sense of familiarity: he becomes both "near and dear" to us. As Rachel Edidin points out in *Wired*, "Cecil himself is at the heart of [*Night Vale*'s] enduring appeal," as well as the focus of the show's avid fan following (Edidin).

Proximity also refers in a more metaphoric sense to *Night Vale*'s characteristic intermingling of the weird and the mundane that comes to us by way of Cecil's narration—the lights of the Arby's and the lights 100 feet above it. In keeping with a primary preoccupation of weird fiction, a genre to which *Night Vale* bears some allegiance, *Night Vale* repeatedly and playfully foregrounds the premise that the universe is a stranger place than we ever imagined, but that the weird is not "out there," not someplace else, but all around us. As Cecil says at the start of episode 69, "Fashion Week," "But don't you see? You never needed anything else. The weird was within you the whole time." The weird, the strange, the other world, the mysteries of the universe are right here with us, as close to us as breathing—just behind that old oak door or unseen in our own home.

Through Cecil's mode of address—the situating of the listener as a Night Vale citizen, the conspiratorial "we," the direct address, the immediacy of voice—we are enfolded into *Night Vale*'s universe of "alternative facts" and inverted logic. This does not mean, however, that we surrender entirely to that logic and forsake the world that we know. We do not merge with Night Vale and, as near and dear as it is to us, we are not residents of the town; rather, although we remain in close proximity to Night Vale, we are nevertheless distanced through the consistent subversion of expectations. We can only ever get so "close" to Night Vale because, in Night Vale, that which we know to be true (the existence of mountains, say) is disputed, while that which we typically reject as absurd or fantastic is often acknowledged as commonplace and common sense—as Wu puts it in the title of her article, Night Vale is a place where "the queer is normal and normal is bizarre" (Wu).

This ironic subversion of expectation is often consciously developed by the program. Consider, for instance, the opening to episode 58, "The Monolith." After cautioning listeners with his opening observation not to jump to conclusions based on appearances ("If it looks like a duck, and it quacks like a duck ... you should not be so quick to jump to conclusions"), Cecil then begins the show proper with what seems like a very ominous report:

> Listeners, someone built a monolith in front of City Hall overnight.
>
> Last night, there was no 15-foot tall, two-foot thick rectangle made of blue slate towering over the faded grass and weakened tulip garden in front of City Hall. But now, there is. A monolith, with indifferent geometry and a long, sharp shadow cast by the low morning sun. It is an ominous construction, channeling ancient powers and long-dead gods. Perhaps, it is even connected to our primordial extra-terrestrial ancestry. And now, just a few days before Christmas, this looming, dark stone shows up mysteriously in the night, casting scornful shadows across both our dreams and our primitive understanding of the world.

Then, however, abruptly changing his tone to a much more affirming one, Cecil concludes, "It's super-festive and I love it! Whoever put that thing up, good job! It must weigh … 20 tons? Don't know how you did it, but way to get us all into the holiday spirit!" Particularly in light of Cecil Baldwin's dramatic delivery of the initial description of the monolith, the unexpected change in tone and ironic inversion of expectations provokes laughter. We should indeed not be so quick to call a duck a duck in Night Vale, and the contradiction of our expectations makes clear that, as much as we may love the program, we are not ourselves Night Valeans.

Much of the humor of *Night Vale* is produced through this form of structural irony created by Cecil's deadpan delivery of the absurd, horrific, fantastic, or downright silly with the tacit assumption that the listener shares this foreign worldview when, of course, we don't. Lights above the Arby's? We know their game. An ominous 20-ton monolith that appears suddenly overnight? How festive! A sentient glowing cloud (all hail!) that runs the School Board? Sure. A Faceless Old Woman Who Lives In Your Home? Of course. Were these events and characters introduced as intrusions into the familiar world of the listener, they would be the stuff of horror—and, indeed, they often retain a kind of residue of the weird and horrific. But because they are regarded by Cecil as the Night Vale norm, we greet them with a startled chuckle—a response also evoked by the series' other comic touches and broader strategy of understatement.

To be fair, a lot of *Night Vale* is played straightforwardly for laughs, which is part of its charm. Consider, for example, some entries from the recurring "community calendar" segment: "Saturday has been merged with Sunday to create Superday! Monday will not harm you, but you should stock up on latex gloves, nevertheless. And Tuesday is hornet-free dining at the Olive Garden" (episode 18, "The Traveler"). Or from the "horoscopes" segment: "*Virgo*: You should check under your bed before you go to sleep. That way the thing hiding in your closet will think you haven't realized where it is yet. *Libra*: All eyes are on you. Gross! Give them back! ... *Cancer*: I'm not saying this is bad news, but the stars just say 'Aaaaaaaaaaaggggghhhhhhhhhh!!!!!!!!!' I mean, maybe that's a good sign, right? Right? It's a very inexact science" (episode 75, "Through the Narrow Place"). Laughter is also evoked in a direct way by silly situations, out-and-out absurdities, and even incongruous names—such as a dog park that neither human beings nor dogs should enter (episode 1, "Pilot"), an 18-foot tall five-headed dragon suspected of insurance fraud and trying to pass himself off as "Frank Chen" (episode 2, "Glow Cloud"), another five-headed dragon—a lawyer no less—named Hadassah McDaniels, and *Night Vale*'s revision to the Boy Scout hierarchy to include Blood Pact Scout, Weird Scout, Dreadnaught Scout, Dark Scout, Fear Scout, and, finally, Eternal Scout (episode 2, "Glow Cloud").

A more pointed form of absurdity is often present in *Night Vale*'s defamiliarization and parodying of the conventions of radio broadcasting. Among the other recurring segments of *Night Vale* are the weather, traffic, and messages from sponsors. As *Night Vale* listeners know, the weather segment always consists of a song and has nothing to do with the weather—this is initially confusing to new *Night Vale* listeners, but we quickly catch on. Traffic, too, as the *Welcome to Night Vale Wiki* summarizes, seldom has anything to do with road conditions and instead "is generally some sort of vignette, often with some sort of vague but bleak existential message" ("Traffic"). A case in point is the end of the traffic report from episode 15, "Street Cleaning Day": "There are several accidents to report. In fact, infinite accidents. Everything is an accident. *Or at least, let us hope so.*" We recognize the content of these segments as bizarre because they parody or subvert familiar radio conventions; as with Cecil's deadpan delivery of his reports about the weirdness of Night Vale, here, too, we as listeners appreciate an ironic incongruity between form and content. It's a bit like a Magritte painting: this is not the traffic, this is not the weather, this is not the Children's Fun Fact Science Corner.

Night Vale's ironic humor is perhaps most apparent however—and rubs up against its politics—in its "a word from our sponsors" segments. While these are sometimes from made-up, ridiculous, or generic sponsors (the physical act of gulping, Venom Box, knife, your mom, a gray pigeon named Alfonso whispering to you from your neighbor's backyard), the majority are attributed to real-world businesses: Coca-Cola, Subway, Target, Home

Depot, Red Lobster, Starbucks, Craigslist, and so on. But in place of empty sloganeering and jingles, *Night Vale* substitutes a warning against wishing for immortality (DirecTV, episode 12, "The Candidate"), a meditation on different types of silence (Target, episode 15, "Street Cleaning Day"), a consideration of the illusion of safety (Denny's, episode 27, "First Date"), and (as the "Welcome to Night Vale Wiki" page on "A Word From Our Sponsors" puts it [see "A Word"]) "an increasingly abstract discussion of abstractions" (Hulu, episode 42, "Numbers"). If the ad spots have anything to do with the business being featured, the association is generally negative—such as the spot for Red Lobster that seemingly puts the listener in the place of the lobster (episode 22, "The Whispering Forest") or the conclusion to a spot for Whole Foods that asks, "Why in the world would we poison our frozen dinners? We definitely do not do that!" (episode 49A, "Old Oak Doors, Part A"). More often, however, the spots seem like *non sequiturs* that make connections on a general level between large corporations and existential angst. The spot for Clorox Bleach in episode 89 ("Who's a Good Boy? Part 1") is exemplary in this respect: "And now, a word from our sponsors: It is possible the world is ending. If you cannot hide, then you must run. If you cannot run, then you must die. This message brought to you by Clorox Bleach."

These spots for corporate sponsors have two important effects within *Night Vale*. First, they serve as an important tether to the "real world." We know that Night Vale has an Arby's and an Olive Garden. And while to the best of our knowledge it lacks a Home Depot, Costco, or Jo-Ann Fabrics, that these companies—along with Coca-Cola, Pfizer, Google, Harper Perennial, and so on—are introduced as sponsors is a sometimes jarring reminder that Night Vale exists as part of the world we know; these references to actual companies and corporations puncture the hermetic bubble around Night Vale, allowing "our world" to seep in.

Second and more importantly, these spots are consistent with and help convey *Night Vale*'s value system, which brings us to among the most interesting issues in relation to *Night Vale*: its function as social critique. While there is a good bit to *Night Vale* that is simply silly or revels in absurdity for the sake of absurdity, the program nevertheless reflects particular orientations and conveys its positions on contemporary political and social issues. In particular, the program resists corporatism and predatory capitalism, and privileges diversity and tolerance. *Night Vale* is unabashedly liberal in its politics, as well as very precise and intentional in its staging of intersections between Night Vale and the "real world." For the most part, Night Vale avoids direct references to contemporary American politics and Night Vale's connection to the real world often seems tenuous—Cecil isn't even sure if the state of Michigan (which he has trouble pronouncing, usually saying it as "Mitch-eye-gan") exists. Then, however, there have been direct jabs at the National Rifle Association. Indeed, in the very first episode, Cecil mentions that the "local chapter of the NRA is selling bumper stickers as a fundraiser with the following slogan: 'Guns don't kill people. It's impossible to be killed by a gun. We are all invincible to bullets and it's a miracle.'" The program then returned to this theme one year later in episode 25 (coincidentally titled "One Year Later") with the following even more pointed report from Cecil:

> The local chapter of the NRA has begun market-testing some possible new slogans. These include:
>
> - Guns don't kill people, blood loss and organ damage does
> - Guns don't kill people, people kill guns
> - A list of things that kill people:
>   1. Conceivably, *anything*
>   2. Not guns!
> - Guns don't kill people, we are all immortal souls living temporarily in shelters of earth and meat
>
> And,
>
> - If you say guns kill people one more time, I will shoot you with a gun, and you will, coincidentally, die
>
> To vote on the new slogan, simply fire a gun at the object or person that best represents your choice.

Night Vale's parodying here of the NRA talking point, "guns don't kill people, people kill people," has the effect of painting the real-world slogan as absurd, and thereby functions as a kind of anti-NRA political intervention. (In the 111th episode celebrating the 6th anniversary of the program ["Summer 2017, Night Vale, USA," aired August 1, 2017], Cecil reprises this message, but with a telling difference: "The local chapter of the NRA is selling bumper stickers as part of their fundraising week. The stickers are made from good sturdy vinyl, and they read, 'We genuinely do not value human life.' Cute!").

To a certain extent, *Night Vale*'s anti-NRA position is congruent with its larger suspicion of administrative structures and large corporations.

While former intern Dana Cardinal (voiced by Jasika Nicole) seems to serve relatively effectively as mayor of Night Vale (despite not having run for the position—the position of mayor, we learn, is, despite votes cast, generally decided by pulses coming from Hidden Gorge [special unnumbered live episode "The Debate"])—station management and the Night Vale town council, in contrast, are presented as being, literally, inhuman (as is the Glow Cloud that presides over the School Board). Night Vale is also of course subject to the whims of the Sheriff's Secret Police, as well as the machinations of the oft-mentioned "vague yet menacing government agency" that sometimes coordinates with the City Council and the Secret Police. Administrative structures in general are parodied by *Night Vale* as both corrupt and inept.

An even more pointed locus of critique developed by *Night Vale* is of corporate capitalism—a position made clear in Cecil's introduction to episode 105, "What Happened at the Smithwick House": "If you could press a button that would give you a great deal of money, but it would cause someone you don't know in a distant part of the world to die, then you would have a good model for how our current economy works." As noted above, the absurdity of the "a word from our sponsors" segments often foregrounds the inherent emptiness and deceptiveness of real-world commercials for big companies and corporations, which try to convince us through carefully crafted messages that their products will fulfill us and that they care about something other than profit. (*Night Vale*'s canniest ad in this respect is their one for Home Depot, which is punctuated repeatedly by the question, "Incomplete?" [episode 19A, "The Sandstorm, Part A"].) This anti-corporate message, however, is developed most fully in the year-two StrexCorp arc. As summarized on the *Welcome to Night Vale Wiki*, StrexCorp Synernists Inc. is "a mysterious private corporation" that runs the neighboring town of Desert Bluffs and that for a short while takes control of Night Vale, leading to a Night Vale rebellion and violent confrontation. "StrexCorp promotes the worship of a 'smiling god,' and routinely releases announcements pressuring citizens to improve their productivity and extend their work hours" ("StrexCorp"). Aside from StrexPets—genetically engineered animal hybrids (one given to Cecil attacks both him and floating men's room cat Khoshekh [episode 43, "Visitor"])—and "transdimensional oranges and orange products" with the "unfortunate side effect of causing customers to cease to exist forever" (episode 38, "Orange Grove"), it is not entirely clear what StrexCorp does; their mind-control program, however, is obvious, as is made clear through their slogan, "Look around you: Strex. Look inside you: Strex. Go to sleep: Strex. Believe in a smiling god. StrexCorp. It is everything" (episode 32, "Yellow Helicopters"). In episode 46, "Parade Day," a failed rebellion against StrexCorp is orchestrated by 13-year-old Tamika Flynn and her child militia. Then, after StrexCorp reveals plans for a "massive renovation" of Night Vale and interns almost all of its citizens, the combined efforts of Night Vale citizens, Angels, and a mysterious masked army from an equally mysterious desert otherworld, StrexCorp is overthrown (episode 49, "Old Oak Doors Part B") and then purchased by the Angels.

Across the series' history, the town of Night Vale has been repeatedly threatened by powerful forces—including a demon in the guise of a beagle puppy, a ferocious sandstorm, angry five-headed dragons, and the unraveling of reality itself brought about by the god Huntokar. And, as noted, the citizens of Night Vale are subject to the whims of various corrupt and inscrutable government agencies. That the single most pernicious force should be a large corporation then is particularly revealing concerning *Night Vale*'s politics. What this seems to suggest is that, more than alien gods and monsters, what we have to fear in the real world is brainwashing by mercenary corporations that worship profit above all else.

However, if *Night Vale* gives us much to fear—both in terms of imaginary and real monsters—as has often been noted in the press, it also provides at the same time a compensatory representation of a world in which diversity of sexuality, ethnicity, and physical ability is both accepted and respected. One of the most notable aspects of *Night Vale* is its straightforward representation of different sexualities. Indeed, in the very first episode of *Night Vale*, Cecil falls head-over-heels in love with scientist Carlos, who has just arrived in Night Vale. "Carlos," explains Cecil, "told us that we are *by far* the most scientifically interesting community in the U.S., and he had come to study just what is going on around here. He grinned, and everything about him was perfect, and I fell in love instantly" (episode 1, "Pilot"). Cecil and Carlos' relationship has been a constant throughout the series, culminating in their wedding in episode 100 ("Toast"). As Cassie Carroll notes in "A Lesson In How Easy Diversity Can Be: 'Welcome to Night Vale'," "Many strange things happen to Cecil and Carlos—angels that don't exist, forests that have a habit of kidnapping people, and old oak doors that lead to desert otherworlds. However, not once, in over four years, has the issue of Cecil and Carlos being queer come up. Nobody has to come out to their parents, no one has to work to get their friends to accept them, they simply live their weird lives, as a same-sex couple" (Carroll). In an interview with *The Advocate*, Dylan Marron, who voices Carlos, explains that "Carlos and Cecil's relationship is the least weird thing about Night Vale ... I think a ton is being said about it by not saying something about it" (Wu). This easy acceptance of diversity in sexuality extends beyond Cecil and Carlos to other characters as well. Episode 79, "Lost in the Mail," is mostly narrated by a character named Basimah Bishara (voiced by Aliee Chan), who tells us in an off-hand way not only that she wears a hijab, but that she has a girlfriend rather than a boyfriend. And, interestingly, Sheriff Sam (voiced by Emma Frankland), who assumes the position in episode 80 ("A New Sheriff in Town"), is referred to exclusively using the gender-neutral pronouns, they, them, and theirs.

Night Vale's "dedication to diversity and inclusiveness," as Wu puts it, extends well beyond sexuality to encompass physical ability and ethnicity. As concerns the differently abled, Cecil's niece, Janice, is in a wheelchair and we learn in episode 110 ("Matryoshka") that she was born with spina bifida and has been unable to walk since birth. However, in episode 49B ("Old Oak Doors Part B"), the suggestion presented by StrexCorp representative Kevin (voiced by Kevin R. Free) that Janice could be healed is angrily rejected by her father, Steve Carlsberg (voiced by Hal Lublin). "Try and tell me there's something about her needs fixin'," says Steve to Cecil after ejecting Kevin through the portal represented by the oak doors. Even more notable for being differently abled are Night Vale residents Michael Sandero and Megan Wallaby. Sandero was the quarterback for the Night Vale High School football team with the unusual feature of having two heads, while Wallaby was a Night Vale elementary school student born as an adult male hand. Wu writes that "Everyone in *Night Vale* accepts Megan's gender identity without question, and the school installs an artificially intelligent supercomputer to allow her to communicate more easily with her peers" (Wu). While this technically isn't true—in episode 34, "A Beautiful Dream," we do learn that Megan has been teased at school due to not having a body, which is what precipitates the request on her parents' part for a computer to help her communicate—nevertheless, she is a valued member of the community who ultimately becomes a "body recipient" and gets grafted onto the body of 6'10" bald Russian man named Nulogorsk. Pushing physical diversity to perhaps its farthest possible extreme are Deb (voiced by Meg Bashwiner), a sentient patch of haze, and Dr. Sarah Sultan, president of Night Vale Community College, who is a smooth, fist-sized river rock and who communicates by sending telepathic messages (episode 50, "Capital Campaign"). What one looks like in Night Vale does not matter. As Baldwin notes in an interview, "The characters in *Night Vale* are not defined by what they look like or their gender or their ethnicity or their physical form." "They're defined by how they treat other people" (Wu).

As concerns ethnic diversity, *Night Vale* clearly makes a substantial effort to include characters whose names and speech patterns suggest diverse backgrounds and ethnicities. Among the register of Night Vale residents are resistance leader and now Town Council member Tamika Flynn, NVPR intern Kareem, high school running back Maliq Herrera, high school football coach Nazr Al-Mujaheed, five-headed dragon Hadassa McDaniels, Dark Owl Records owner Michelle Nguyen, and resident Roger Singh (described on his wiki page as a Sikh [see "Roger Singh"]). And beyond including these characters, *Night Vale* has made a concerted effort to have characters voiced by actors whose identities correspond to those of the characters. Along these lines, an important shift was made by the program in its first season when *Night Vale* switched the voice of Carlos from creator Jeffrey Cranor to Dylan Marron. About the switch, Cranor explained on Tumblr that:

> It sucks that there's a white straight male (me), playing a gay man of color (Carlos). Look, I know it's a voiceover, but it's not just that. We do live stage shows, and that's a visible role for a PoC. Plus, fans often google the actors who play each character, and what does a Latino/Latina teen think when my face might pop up (or worse, no image pops up) as the actor playing Carlos? What am I doing voicing this major character when there are so many talented, gay, Latino or Hispanic men who can/should be doing it? Why didn't I think of all of this before ep 16? I don't know.
>
> But here I am: standing in the way of a actor of color getting paid acting work, and I don't want to do that since I am neither a PoC nor an actor. ("ch-ch-ch-ch-changes")

As Carroll suggests, *Night Vale*'s commitment to inclusivity, both in terms of its characters and its actors, seems a sincere effort to reflect the diversity of the world in which we live rather than to tick off boxes, while attempting at the same time to offer a picture of how the world could be if individuals were people defined not be sexuality or physical ability or ethnicity but by personal character. *Night Vale* for Carroll is an example of how a program can include diversity without making difference from the white, heterosexual, conventionally able-bodied norm the defining feature of characters. This "intelligent attitude toward the fact of human diversity" (Baker-Whitelaw) has clearly been an important element of the podcast's success. As Wu explains, "Welcome to Night Vale's dedication to diversity and inclusiveness and its strong writing have earned it massively enthusiastic audiences both online and at live shows" (Wu). She continues, "Many teenagers, especially those who identify as LGBT, find refuge in Night Vale, where even the strangest characters and events can be commonplace. 'We get a lot of people, teenagers, preteens, that have written us and told us in person that as somebody who is gay or understands themselves as genderqueer or gender-fluid or transgender, they feel comfort in our show that they don't feel in a lot of other places, and they feel normal,' says Cranor." Rendering queer as normal thus has the effect of queering our own world, in the sense of foregrounding exclusionary norms and discriminatory practices that alienate and disenfranchise those whose identities and appearances diverge from socially constructed but nevertheless deeply embedded standards. Put differently, nowhere is *Night Vale*'s critique of the real world more apparent than in its representation of an alternate world that seems Utopian to many because of its open acceptance of diversity.

Which brings us then to this volume, a labor of love on the part of a group of "acafans," to use the term popularized by Matt Hills in his 2002 study *Fan Cultures* for scholars who are fans of that which they study, who feel that *Welcome to Night Vale* is important and merits close attention. As you will see, the inclusions here expand on many of the themes of this introduction. Dawn Stobbart, Danielle Hancock, and Heidi Lyn consider the program's politics of representation and fan response. Andy McCumber focuses on the construction of Night Vale as a place. Grace Gist and Michael Patrick Vaughn explore aspects of Cecil with attention to issues of intimacy, distance, and memory. Elliott Freeman thinks about *Night Vale* as poetry. And rounding out the collection is Line Henriksen's meditation on the ways in which *Night Vale* confronts us with the void and what good could perhaps come from this.

From the Arby's to the lights above them, and from the weather to the void, *Welcome to Night Vale* takes us on a trip in several directions at once—to a small desert town where all conspiracy theories are true, to a nightmarish otherworld that is simultaneously liberating, back in time to older forms of media, forward in time to where media is heading, and to the cusp of the void. *Night Vale* has much to say to us and the contributors to this collection are ready to explore what it says, how it says it, what it means, and why it is important. But perhaps Cecil sums things up best in the introduction to episode 9 ("Pyramid"): "Weird at last! Weird at last! God Almighty, weird at last! Welcome to Night Vale."

WORKS CITED

"A Word From Our Sponsors." *Welcome to Night Vale Wiki.* Accessed July 13, 2017. http://nightvale.wikia.com/wiki/A_Word_From_Our_Sponsors.

Baker-Whitelaw, Gavia. "In the Surreal Shadows of 'Night Vale,' a New Fandom Lurks." *The Daily Dot,* 23 July 2013. Accessed July 12, 2017. https://www.dailydot.com/parsec/fandom/welcome-night-vale-podcast-fandom/.

Barton, Chris. "Review 'Welcome to Night Vale' Podcast Becomes an Equally Weird, Haunted Yet Humorous Novel." *Los Angeles Times,* 16 October 2015. Accessed July 12, 2017. http://www.latimes.com/books/jacketcopy/la-ca-jc-1018-night-vale-20151018-story.html.

Bottomley, Andrew J. "Podcasting, *Welcome to Night Vale,* and the Revival of Radio Drama." *Journal of Radio & Audio Media* 22, no. 2 (2015): 179–189.

Carlson, Adam. "America's Most Popular Podcast: What the Internet Did to 'Welcome to Night Vale'." *The Awl,* 24 July 2013. Accessed July 13, 2017. https://theawl.com/americas-most-popular-podcast-what-the-internet-did-to-welcome-to-night-vale-ba78f910fe2.

Carroll, Cassie. "A Lesson in How Easy Diversity Can Be: 'Welcome to Night Vale'." *TheOdysseyOnline.com,* 25 July 2016. Accessed July 13, 2017. https://www.theodysseyonline.com/lesson-easy-diversity-night-vale.

Cranor, Jeffrey. "ch-ch-ch-ch-Changes, or: Who Is Carlos?" *happierman.net,* 2014. Accessed July 13, 2017. http://happierman.tumblr.com/post/69936379508/ch-ch-ch-ch-changes-or-who-is-carlos.

———. "Introduction." In *The Great Glowing Coils of the Universe: Welcome to Night Vale,* ed. Joseph Fink and Jeffrey Cranor, xiii–xvi. New York: Harper Perennial, 2016.

D'Amico, Anthony. "Celebrating Their Corpse-Strewn Future: Welcome to Night Vale." *Brainwashed,* 26 May 2013. Accessed July 13, 2017. http://brainwashed.com/index.php?option=com_content&view=article&id=9689:welcome-to-night-vale-part-one&catid=74:interviews&Itemid=91.

Edidin, Rachel. "*Welcome to Night Vale,* the #1 Podcast on Itunes You Didn't Know Existed." *Wired,* 21 August 2013. Accessed July 12, 2017. https://www.wired.com/2013/08/night-vale-podcast-itunes/.

Fink, Joseph. "Introduction." In *Mostly Void, Partially Stars: Welcome to Night Vale Episodes, Volume 1,* ed. Joseph Fink and Jeffrey Cranor, xvii–xx. London: Harper Perennial, 2016.

Fink, Joseph, and Jeffrey Cranor. *Great Glowing Coils of the Universe: Welcome to Night Vale Episodes, Volume 2.* New York: Harper Perennial, 2016a.

————. *Mostly Void, Partially Stars: Welcome to Night Vale Episodes, Volume 1.* London: Harper Perennial, 2016b.

Hills, Matt. *Fan Cultures.* London: Routledge, 2002.

Maksym, Eileen. "Lake Wobegon Meets H.P. Lovecraft: Welcome to Night Vale." *Various and Sundry: The World and Writing of Eileen Maksym*, 15 October 2015. Accessed July 12, 2017. https://eileenmaksym.com/2015/10/15/lake-wobegon-meets-h-p-lovecraft-welcome-to-night-vale/.

"Roger Singh." *Welcome to Night Vale Wiki.* Accessed July 13, 2017. http://nightvale.wikia.com/wiki/Roger_Singh.

Rugnetta, Mike. "How Does Night Vale Confront Us with the Unknown?" PBS Idea Channel, *YouTube*, 25 September 2013. https://www.youtube.com/watch?v=Jg7ktpew2Tc.

"Strexcorp Synernists Incorporated." *Welcome to Night Vale Wiki.* Accessed July 13, 2017. http://nightvale.wikia.com/wiki/StrexCorp_Synernists_Incorporated.

Virtue, Graeme. "Welcome to Night Vale, the Podcast That's Like a Local News Twin Peaks." *theguardian.com*, 14 March 2014. Accessed July 13, 2017. https://www.theguardian.com/tv-and-radio/2014/mar/14/night-vale-podcast?CMP=share_btn_link.

Weber, Lindsey. "Night Vale Creators Joseph Fink and Jeffrey Cranor Explain Their Cultural Influences." *Vulture: Devouring Culture*, 7 November 2013. Accessed July 13, 2017. http://www.vulture.com/2013/10/cultural-influences-of-night-vales-creators.html.

"Welcome to 'Night Vale'—Watch Out for the Tarantulas." *NPR.org*, 31 August 2013. Accessed July 12, 2017. http://www.npr.org/2013/08/31/216865781/welcome-to-night-vale-watch-out-for-the-tarantulas.

Wu, Connie. "Welcome to Night Vale: Where Queer Is Normal and Normal Is Bizarre." *The Advocate*, 26 September 2014. Accessed July 13, 2017. https://www.advocate.com/arts-entertainment/2014/09/29/welcome-night-vale-where-queer-normal-and-normal-bizarre.

CHAPTER 2

"Everything About Him Was Just Perfect. And I Fell in Love Instantly": Life and Love in *Welcome to Night Vale*

Dawn Stobbart

Abstract Despite, or even because of, its surreal and fantastical characters, Night Vale is an open and accepting place for most of its residents, and using the podcasts and the 2015 novel, this chapter explores Night Vale's ability to accept diversity. Focusing on representations of gender, sexuality, and disability, I show Night Vale to be an open-minded, progressive town, and that the podcast actively endorses attitudes of acceptance and understanding, not only through the actions of the characters affected by these issues, but by the actions of the inhabitants themselves, particularly radio host Cecil, and how they treat each other.

Keywords Cecil • Carlos • Disability • Diversity • Gender neutrality • Josh Crayton • Megan Wallaby • Racism • Sexuality • Whitewashing

D. Stobbart (✉)
Lancaster University, Lancaster, UK

© The Author(s) 2018
J. A. Weinstock (ed.), *Critical Approaches to* Welcome to Night Vale,
https://doi.org/10.1007/978-3-319-93091-6_2

In December 2016, *Welcome to Night Vale* celebrated its 100th installment with an episode entitled "Toast." Featuring all of the voices that have appeared in *Night Vale* since its inception in June 2012, "Toast" is a celebration of the show and of the relationship between radio host Cecil Palmer and scientist Carlos as they get married. *Welcome to Night Vale*, as the chapters in this volume will attest, allows listeners to follow the rather strange, surreal, and sometimes pedestrian experiences of a community living in "a small desert town somewhere in the Southwestern United States." Night Vale is described as "the most scientifically interesting community in the US" (Fink and Cranor, *Mostly Void* 5), and the podcast routinely shows this to be true; delivered in twice-monthly installments, the podcast is framed through the voice of Night Vale public radio host Cecil Palmer as he conveys local news and happenings to the community, making them seem normal, and even mundane.

While Night Vale is a place where strange events are commonplace and conspiracy theories are an accepted reality, it is also a place where "people" are accepted for who they are, whether that is a sentient patch of haze named Deb, or a glowing cloud that is the head of the Parent-Teachers Association (PTA). This acceptance is shown during the pilot episode when Cecil describes the first time he sees Carlos, saying "he grinned and everything about him was perfect, and I fell in love instantly" (Fink and Cranor, *Mostly Void* 5). Cecil is from the outset established as a gay character; however, this is not the defining characteristic of Cecil, an unusual (but not unknown) stance in most media: Frederik Dhaenens cites several changes that have taken place in television production in his analysis of the television show *Glee*, for example (Dhaenens). But, as Cecil Baldwin, the voice of Cecil Palmer, says in an interview, this is still far from usual as

> [m]ainstream media has a tendency to let "gay" or "lesbian" or "transgender" be that defining characteristic of characters without showing audiences the person beyond that. We're more interested in showing our characters as whole people, especially those in a long-term relationship with its rewards and flaws and every silly, boring thing that makes love so beautiful. (Butcher)

In this chapter, I focus on how *Welcome to Night Vale* presents a community that accepts the diversity in its inhabitants but also consider how it endorses attitudes of acceptance and understanding through the actions of the inhabitants themselves, particularly radio host Cecil, and how they treat each other. To do this, I will primarily use the podcast episodes, with reference to the 2015 novel, *Welcome to Night Vale* by Fink and Cranor, to consider the representations of gender, sexuality, and disability as they appear in the fictional community.

In the introduction to the second volume of *Welcome to Night Vale* transcripts, *The Great Glowing Coils of the Universe*, Cranor explains some of the reasons that he thinks *Welcome to Night Vale* has become such a success. These reasons include the release of episode 27: "First Date." Regular listeners of the podcast had been privy to Cecil's feelings toward Carlos the Scientist since the first episode "Pilot," where, as cited earlier, Cecil relates his feelings toward the scientist that arrives in Night Vale, but these feelings do not appear to be reciprocated until the end of episode 25: "One Year Later." It was at about this point in the podcast that listening figures rose exponentially. The first year saw *Welcome to Night Vale* being downloaded approximately 150,000 times over 25 episodes; in the 13th month (2 episodes)—which includes "First Date"—this number grew to 2.5 million (Fink and Cranor, *Coils* xiv). It is in this episode that listeners become privy to "the culmination of the relationship between host Cecil Palmer and Carlos the scientist" (Fink and Cranor, *Coils* xv), and which deviated from the norm in mainstream fiction. The key difference between this same-sex relationship and others in popular fiction, according to Cranor, is that in most of the mainstream media, viewers, readers, and listeners engage with a "teased-out, will-they-won't-they, same-sex relationship," where "couples are drawn close but never allowed to get together as a loving couple" (Fink and Cranor, *Coils* xvi). *Welcome to Night Vale* instead challenges heteronormative behavior by presenting "a couple that falls in love without getting hung up on outdated hetero-assumptive conditions" (Fink and Cranor, *Coils* xvi)—assumptions that include the understanding that "if you are born with male genitalia ... you will behave in masculine ways, desire women ... have sex in what are thought to be normally active and insertive ways and within officially sanctioned contexts" (Warner 37). It is interesting to note that not one character in more than four years has mentioned Cecil and Carlos being part of a *same-sex* relationship, even though Cecil openly discusses his relationship in most of the podcast episodes, supporting the concept of an open and accepting community.

Media that caters to the gay community sees the podcast as being actively supportive of diversity in all forms; an interview in *The Advocate*, an American LGTB interest magazine, reports that "*Welcome to Night Vale* has created a home for listeners of all different identities, ethnicities, and orientations," with "the relationship between Cecil ... and Carlos" (Wu) taking the center stage of the podcast. The article notes that while audiences "have made a big deal over each romantic gesture, the citizens of

Night Vale … couldn't care less that their community radio host is in a gay relationship." Dylan Marron, who provides the voice of Carlos concurs, remarking in the same interview, that "Carlos and Cecil's relationship is the least weird thing about Night Vale" (Wu)—and with the presence of five-headed dragons, secret police, and a faceless old woman who lives in your home, this statement is, without a doubt, true. The normativity of their relationship is highlighted throughout the podcast; the bond between the two characters is realistic in its depictions of their interactions with— and about—each other, and they deal with the same issues present in any relationship, such as "negotiating schedules and habits that just sort of irk you about your partner" (Adri). Showing the relationship as being just like any other allows listeners (some of whom may be struggling to understand their own sexuality) to think of same-sex relationships in a healthy way, and furthermore allows listeners who (may) have only been exposed to negative depictions of same-sex relationships to view them as normal— with the same challenges and highlights as any other. This is important; young people especially "are faced with a continual barrage of prejudicial ideology they hear too often" (Goldman 34) and are expected to "assume positions that are centered around the nuclear family and which are gendered, sexualized, and fixed in time and space" (Dhaenens 306). *Welcome to Night Vale* offers an alternative viewpoint, one that espouses openness and equality for all people, without the heteronormative agenda of "reproduction, marriage, and longevity" (Dhaenens 306).

In episode 79, "Lost in the Mail" (Vee), Basimah Bishara shares her memories of her father, who left to fight in a space war and is able to send home one letter per year. Most of the letters are, she says, "lists of ways I need to live my life," including the need to wear her hijab (which she does for mosque, but not often at school) and "not to kiss a boy until I was 16" (Vee), to which she interjects, "well, I guess good news for him there," as she has "a girlfriend not a boyfriend." As with Cecil and Carlos, Basimah does not need to state explicitly that she is gay, just as she doesn't explicitly state that she is Muslim; both of these things are just part of her life, aspects of her personality that are just that—aspects. Just as—or even more—important than her sexuality and ethnicity is the fact that her father is away at war and as such is missing most of her childhood, not knowing, for example, that she spent most of her 14th year recovering from a car accident. Once again, the podcast iterates that the sexuality of a character is. merely part of their make-up and that there are other defining things that construct a person.

When *Night Vale* first introduced Carlos the scientist as a speaking character, he was voiced by series writer Jeffrey Cranor (a straight, white actor). However, in the first live performance of the podcast, "Condos," a new actor was introduced to play the role, one more in keeping with the characters ethnic and sexual identity. Although the narrative is delivered primarily from the perspective of Cecil, the live shows, and the large online fandom of *Night Vale* that had come into being by this time, led Cranor to reconsider his involvement as Carlos. In the introduction to episode 16, "The Phone Call," Cranor explains why he made the change: "Not casting white people in roles for people of color is the correct thing to do. It's not a noble or laudable thing to do. It is what you are supposed to do, so we corrected this, by casting a person of color in the role" (Fink and Cranor, *Mostly Void* 140–41). Recent years have seen a controversy surrounding "racebent" or "whitewashed" casting, in which a white actor is cast in the role of a previously non-white character. Examples of this include the actress Scarlet Johansson playing the Japanese character The Major, Motoko Kusanagi, in *The Ghost in the Shell* (Sanders), adapted from the Anime series of the same name, or Benedict Cumberbatch playing the role of Asian character Khan Noonien Singh in *Star Trek 2: Into Darkness* (Abrams), and even straight actor Eddie Redmayne in the role of trans character Einar Wegener in *The Danish Girl* (Hooper). In choosing actors that resemble the characters they are playing, Fink and Cranor acknowledge the inherent discrimination in foregrounding white, heterosexual actors, when there are actors who are better suited to the roles, such as Dylan Marron who is a gay person of color—perfectly suited to play the role of Carlos, also a person of color who identifies as gay. As it does with sexuality, *Welcome to Night Vale* challenges behavior that discriminates against minorities, using actors that reflect the ethnicity of the character they are playing.

As shown earlier, many of the central aspects of *Welcome to Night Vale* were introduced in the first episode. As well as introducing the main characters of the podcast and an openly gay character in the main role, "Pilot" also establishes Night Vale as a place that is open to the presence of characters that might be described in popular fiction as "other"—those who "are everything that lies outside" (Moosavinia, Lorestan, and Ahmad 105) of the (hetero) normative self. There are hooded figures that the listener is asked not to approach or look at; there are angels living "out near the car lot" (Fink and Cranor, *Mostly Void* 3) with Old Woman Josie (although the Night Vale City Council are quick to remind listeners that angels do not exist), and there is a faceless old woman who lives in your home—all of whom are accepted as Night Vale residents. This openness does not come at the cost of accepting negative behaviors however. Night Vale will not accept racism, for example, as can be seen through the presence of The Indian Tracker. This character is described as being of "maybe Slavic origin, yet [he] wears an Indian headdress out of some racist cartoon" (Fink and Cranor, *Mostly Void* 6). His actions and beliefs are quickly shown to be intolerable when Cecil reports that "it's really hard to take him seriously in that headdress" (Fink and Cranor, *Mostly Void* 7). The racist overtones of the character (referred to after the pilot episode as the Apache Tracker) continue throughout the first year of the podcast, as does the refutation of the character's actions. In episode 7, "History Week," Cecil remarks for example that, "I think I speak for everyone in the community when I say good riddance to that local embarrassment. He made the whole town look ignorant and racist" (Fink and Cranor, *Mostly Void* 59). Even when he is transformed into a Native American (who speaks Russian), he is still considered an "asshole"—just because he now wears the correct skin, his past indiscretions do not pardon him, and he is rightly treated as an outcast for his racism. In his final appearance, episode 25, "One Year Later," he is considered to be a "real racist jerk and no one likes him. ... He is the same embarrassment to our town he always was" (Fink and Cranor, *Mostly Void* 249).

However, even he is redeemed. When Carlos is wounded by tiny people who live in a city under the bowling alley, it is the Apache Tracker that rushes to save him, being mortally wounded in the process. After his death, Cecil comments, "How could I have been so wrong about this man? An embarrassment to our town? Maybe. A real jerk? Yes. But he was also a man with Night Vale's best interests at heart ... And he, at the cost of his own life, saved Carlos ... Tell me nothing else, and I will still tell you: Here is a good man" (Fink and Cranor, *Mostly Void* 253–54). His sacrifice is rewarded with the erection of a monument, but this is tempered by it being "buried somewhere in the desert where no one will find it, because he was also a racist embarrassment and we don't want our town associated with that kind of thing" (Fink and Cranor, *Coils* 16). Throughout this story arc, using this character as an example, it is clear that the inhabitants of Night Vale are not willing to condone racism. But, by redeeming him through his sacrifice, they also acknowledge that racism is not the only defining characteristic of the tracker, or of any individual, just as happens with other themes running through the podcast.

The tracker is shown to be a loyal inhabitant of the town, despite their rejection of his beliefs, and honored as a hero for his sacrifice. Even the worst people, the episode tells the reader, can have qualities that show them in a positive light—although, some things cannot be forgotten, even with the ultimate sacrifice.

In episode 18, "The Traveler," Cecil congratulates Tock Wallaby and his wife Hershel on the birth of their daughter Megan, who has been born as "an adult man's hand" (Fink and Cranor, *Mostly Void* 167). Megan Wallaby is a character that reappears in episodes 34, "A Beautiful Dream," and 40, "The Deft Bowman." These episodes reveal a complex, surreal story arc, which raises valid points about the treatment of disability in the real world. Everyone accepts Megan's gender identity without question; despite having the physical form of a male, adult hand, she is a female person. However, her disadvantaged position as a disabled person is highlighted in episode 34, when Cecil reports live from the Night Vale Elementary School, where the PTA have been meeting with the School Board. Firstly, the broad implications of disability are foregrounded when it is reported that "the School Board was ... apathetic to petitions for a wheelchair ramp ... citing perilous struggles as one of the lessons children must absorb" (Fink and Cranor, *Coils* 85), before Megan's parents request that a new computer be bought to assist their daughter, as "she is teased so much at school for not having a body" (Fink and Cranor, *Coils* 86). While the disability Megan has been given in the podcast is absurd, the message behind it is not. The school installs an artificially intelligent computer to allow Megan to communicate with her peers and to help her not feel so alone. As is usual in Night Vale, things go wrong, and the computer must be deactivated, leaving Megan once again alone, imitating the real-life situation of children across the world that cannot join in with their peers due to a disability. Reflecting the levels of discrimination and isolation in the real world, Cecil tells listeners, "There are children in wheelchairs who cannot get a simple ramp at a charter school. ... Likewise, there is a girl who is only a hand, and she needs a computer to help her be part of our community" (Fink and Cranor, *Coils* 93–94). Juxtaposing the absurd with the real, Cecil reminds us (as the listeners in the real world) that discrimination is not confined to a character in a fictional podcast radio show, but rather is something that exists in the twenty-first century, and in places that consider themselves advanced, such as the US and the UK, where these problems should not exist anymore.

Just as sexuality does not define Cecil and Carlos, disability does not define characters in Night Vale. While Megan is noteworthy for her physical differences, she is not the only character in Night Vale that has a disability: Cecil's niece Janice is a wheelchair user. This detail is introduced in episode 49, "Old Oak Doors," a two-part episode, when Steve Carlsberg, (Cecil's brother-in-law and Janice's stepfather), is considering moving to nearby town Desert Bluffs. When he inquires about schools for Janice, he is told by StrexCorp employee Kevin that "Desert Bluffs schools are top-notch! Young Janice can take college prep courses as early as 12. Our charter schools even have great medical programs, where they can heal her of all her problems" (Fink and Cranor, *Coils* 263). The "problems" Kevin is referring to is Janice's wheelchair use, stating that, "rather than build all those crazy ramps and elevators, we just fix people, so that they can become better, and more productive" (Fink and Cranor, *Coils* 263). Again, this is reflective of real life: "[N]early every culture," write David Mitchell and Sharon Snyder in their seminal text *Narrative Prosthesis: Disability and the Dependencies of Discourse*, "views disability as a problem in need of a solution" (Mitchell and Snyder 48), a concept reflected in the words of Kevin, but which are refuted by Steve Carlsberg through his response: "Kevin of Desert Bluffs, you will not change, or fix, or do anything at all to my little girl" (Fink and Cranor, *Coils* 264). Although Janice had appeared in several episodes of *Welcome to Night Vale* prior to this, her disability has been treated in the same way that the relationship between Carlos and Cecil is—completely unremarked upon until it becomes relevant; Janice is defined by who she is, not by the wheelchair she sits in.

The refutation of disability being the defining aspect of a person is taken further in episode 40, "The Deft Bowman," when the story arc surrounding Megan is completed, and she is given a body in the form of an unidentified man with a missing left hand, who offers to donate his own body to allow Megan to live "in the body she was born without" (Fink and Cranor, *Coils* 158). Once again, Cecil reminds the listener of the importance of compassion and understanding, saying that after successful surgery, "Megan has a long road of therapy ahead of her, learning how to … everything … but we believe in her, don't we Night Vale? That little girl is going to enjoy the childhood she feels she has missed out on … If this is what she wants, we will support her, because she is beautiful" (Fink and Cranor, *Coils* 155). Here, as elsewhere in *Welcome to Night Vale*, the listener is reminded that behind every disability there is a person. Whether that person has the form of an adult hand or is a wheelchair user, there is a human being with feelings—one who deserves compassion, under-standing, and most of all support to become the person they want to be.

As well as highlighting the normativity of Carlos and Cecil's relation-ship, and identifying Megan as a girl (rather than having the gender of her body forced on her), *Welcome to Night Vale* seeks to show an equal level of understanding to other minority or discriminated people (a position elab-orated in the novel as well). Just as the podcast allows characters to have disabilities, or be LGBT, and it is simply one of many things that make up each character, individuals in Night Vale are able to explore their own sense of identity before deciding who they want to be, rather than being "forced to embody a fixed sexual identity" (Dhaenens 306) as happens in the real world. This is achieved in several ways, including having characters that are given a gender-neutral pronoun, such as Sheriff Sam. Gender-neutral pronouns are becoming increasingly common, as people are able to openly identify themselves in any way they want to. Sam is referred to as "them" and "they" throughout the podcast and is voiced (and acted in the live shows) by trans actor Emma Frankland. Sheriff Sam has never been referred to by a gendered pronoun, and this gender neutrality allows the podcast to acknowledge the change in how personal pronouns are used. Linda D. Wayne sees gendered terminology as part of a problem that has "devoured our young not only through on-going violence, but though our failure to acknowledge that it consumes the spirit of those who do not fit within its confines" (Wayne 89). This is something that *Welcome to Night Vale* is not only aware of but takes pains to refute. The presence of characters that are spoken of via a gender-neutral personal pronoun or by a gendered term that does not correspond to the physical make-up of a body shows this to good effect.

While acknowledging that the concept of gender is a complicated and deeply personal thing, *Welcome to Night Vale* recognizes the difficulty in exploring identity, and this can be seen in the novel *Welcome to Night Vale: A Novel* through the introduction of a teenage character named Josh Crayton. Josh is a 15-year-old boy, who can take any shape he wants, including "a curve-billed thrasher, or a kangaroo, or a Victorian-era wardrobe," and, "like most teenagers, he always was what he happens to be in that moment, until he never was that" (Fink and Cranor, *Night Vale* 15). While the concept of a young person who can morph into any shape he desires is an exaggerated metaphor for being a teenager, the novel offers this as a way to understand the feelings of both being a teen-ager and of being the parent of a teenager. Just as Night Vale enables dif-ference in adults, children in Night Vale are able to explore their own sense of identity and decide for themselves who they want to be. This includes not only representations of gender, but also of sexuality. Josh is not given a sexuality in the novel, be that gay, straight, trans, or bi. The novel states that, "there was a girl Josh liked, who only liked Josh when he was bipedal" (Fink and Cranor, *Night Vale* 15–16), and that, "there was a boy Josh liked, who only liked Josh when he was a cute animal" (Fink and Cranor, *Night Vale* 16). When he talks to his mother about dating, there is mention of both boys and girls that Josh has been (or is) interested in (Fink and Cranor, *Night Vale* 143), but as with all other instances of sexuality, this is presented as being the norm—Josh is not pressured to fit into a pre-existing notion of gender and sexuality; unlike the real world as Dhaenens (306) explains, in Night Vale, there is no mold to fit into. Equally, in the same conversation, when Diane tells Josh she is dating Dawn, it is not a revelation of her sexuality, merely part of the discussion about dating. As Basimah Bishara says in episode 79, "Everyone's got their own thing, you know? ... So long as you are loved, it doesn't matter" (Vee).

Night Vale's emphasis on inclusivity thus extends to gender as well. While approximately half of the inhabitants of the world are (or identify as) female, there is "a pattern of gender hierarchy [that] has remained in which men continue to be advantaged not only in employment but also throughout much of society" (Ridgeway 1). Men occupy many of the most powerful positions in business and government across the world. The UN Women website states that, "22.8 per cent of all national parliamentarians were women, as of June 2016" (UN Women). Even when women are given positions of power, the media are sometimes more interested in how they appear than how they perform in their role. This is not the case in Night Vale, where female characters outnumber males in terms of their authority. The current Night Vale Mayor is Dana Cardinal, who succeeded Mayor Pamela Winchell—and one of the candidates in the election that elected Dana was the Faceless Old Woman Who Lives in Your Home. Sixteen-year-old Tamika Flynn is considered by Cecil and Dana to be a hero, who led a guerrilla army against corporate giant StrexCorp when they attempted to take over Night Vale. She is also a member of the Night Vale City Council, having appointed herself on her 16th birthday. Dana Cardinal has faced opposition in her time as Mayor, such as an assassination attempt by Hiram McDaniels (a literal five-headed dragon) after her victory in the elections. What is important to note about these characters is that no one in Night Vale has any problems with there being several females in powerful positions; it is never mentioned, and unlike real-world politics, there is no running commentary on the clothes the characters wear, whether they are suitable for the job they have, or whether personal circumstances will mean that they cannot perform their tasks, as has been the case in mainstream media news outlets regarding prominent female politicians across the world. As is the case with each of the concepts examined in this chapter, the creators of *Welcome to Night Vale* are producing a fictional world that places the rights of the individual to be whomever they want to over those who want to enforce stereotypes, and recognizes that a person's worth does not depend on what they look like, who they love, or whether their inner identity matches that which the world sees.

The depiction of sexuality, gender, and identity in *Welcome to Night Vale* is an ideal, expressing the creators' vision of how media should be portraying characters. There are gay people, and as such there should be gay characters in fiction. But being gay should not be the defining characteristic of a person, just as being Muslim or Hispanic or even white should not be. Equally, a disability should not be the first thing that is associated with a person; there should be representations of people in wheelchairs, as this reflects reality. Equally, these depictions should not be plot points, or a way to include minorities, and this is what *Night Vale* excels at: representing people as equal, regardless of their individual characteristics. Most of the time, the listener is given information about a character through Cecil, and his descriptions do not usually include what the character looks like, until it becomes relevant; even Cecil himself is ambiguous. Other than his relationship with Carlos defining him as gay, there is very little description of him as a person; there are no clarifications of his ethnicity or race for example. It is refreshing and heartening for a work of fiction to display a society where homophobia seemingly does not exist, and where cultural appropriation is treated with the contempt it deserves, and where each person is given the freedom to be who they want to be.

WORKS CITED

Adri, M. "Interview: Cecil Baldwin and Jeffrey Cranor of 'Welcome to Night Vale'." October 31, 2013. *newnownext.com*. Accessed January 4, 2017. http://www.newnownext.com/cecil-baldwin-jeffrey-cranor-welcome-to-night-vale/10/2013/.
Butcher, Ryan. "Welcome to Night Vale's Cecil Baldwin: 'Young People Use Night Vale to Begin the Conversation About Their Own Sexuality'." September 25,

2015. *Gaytimes.co.uk*. Accessed December 28, 2016. http://www.gaytimes. co.uk/culture/9151/welcome-to-night-vales-cecil-baldwin-young-people-use-night-vale-to-begin-the-conversation-about-their-own-sexuality/.

Dhaenens, Frederik. "Teenage Queerness: Negotiating Heteronormativity in the Representation of Gay Teenagers in Glee." *Journal of Youth Studies* 16, no. 3 (2013): 304–317. PDF.

Fink, Joseph, and Jeffrey Cranor. *Welcome to Night Vale: A Novel*. London: Orbit, 2015.

———. *Mostly Void, Partially Stars: Welcome to Night Vale Episodes, Volume 1*. London: Harper Perennial, 2016a.

———. *The Great Glowing Coils of the Universe*. New York: Harper Collins, 2016b.

Goldman, Linda. *Coming Out, Coming In: Nurturing the Well-Being and Inclusion of Gay Youth*. Abingdon: Routledge, 2008. Print.

Mitchell, David T., and Sharon L. Snyder. *Narrative Prosthesis: Disability and the Dependencies of Discourse*. Ann Arbor, MI: University of Michigan Press, 2001.

Moosavinia, S.R., N. Niazi Lorestan, and Ghaforian Ahmad. "Edward Said's Orientalism and the Study of the Self and the Other in Orwell's Burmese Days." *Studies in Literature and Language* 2, no. 1 (2011): 102–113. PDF.

Ridgeway, Cecilia L. *Framed by Gender: How Gender Inequality Persists in the Modern World*. Oxford: Oxford University Press, 2011. Print.

UN Women. "Facts and Figures: Leadership and Political Participation." August 2016. *UN Women*. Accessed January 5, 2017. http://www.unwomen.org/en/what-we-do/leadership-and-political-participation/facts-and-figures.

Vee, Kenny. "Cecil Speaks: Episode 79 Lost in the Mail." November 30, 2015. *Tumblr*. Accessed January 4, 2017. http://cecilspeaks.tumblr.com/post/134320284811/episode-79-lost-in-the-mail.

Warner, Michael. *The Trouble with Normal: Sex, Politics, and the Ethics of Queer Life*. New York: The Free Press, 1999. Print.

Wayne, Linda D. "Neutral Pronouns: A Modest Proposal Whose Time Has Come." *Canadian Woman Studies* 24, no. 2 (2005). PDF.

Wu, Connie. "Welcome to Night Vale: Where Queer Is Normal and Normal Is Bizarre." September 29, 2014. *The Advocate*. Accessed January 2, 2017. http://www.advocate.com/arts-entertainment/2014/09/29/welcome-night-vale-where-queer-normal-and-normal-bizarre.

CHAPTER 3

Our Friendly Desert Town: Alternative Podcast Culture in *Welcome to Night Vale*

Danielle Hancock

Abstract Despite its frequently horrific context, *Night Vale*'s community aspect represents one of its most-loved facets, with fans embracing and developing the show's fantasy of shared location, listenership, and identity. This chapter posits that *Night Vale* fans build and experience traditionalistic forms of community through imagined and performed "Night Vale" residence and community "radio" listenership; collective visual construction and definition of *Night Vale*'s invisible spaces and inhabitants; and communication and collectivism enacted both as "cyber" and physically co-present audiences. In these three elements of reception, *Night Vale* may realize fresh potential for new audio-media and expose alternate desires in audio-media users, as with each "broadcast" fans continue to cultivate old modes of community, traditionalism, and collectivity in very new ways.

Keywords Community • Fandom • Otherness • Place • Podcast

D. Hancock (✉)
University of East Anglia, Norwich, UK
e-mail: HancockD@regents.ac.uk

© The Author(s) 2018
J. A. Weinstock (ed.), *Critical Approaches to* Welcome to Night Vale,
https://doi.org/10.1007/978-3-319-93091-6_3

Podcasts, alongside their iPod namesakes, are often charged with promoting antisocial tendencies. Headphones, earbuds, playlists, and on-demand listening seemingly foster disconnection both from listeners' surrounding physical world and from the connective, collective ties of traditional live radio (Lacey; Levy; Bull). Thus, new audio-media is understood as both eliciting and exemplary of contemporary breakdowns in traditional societal values. The iPod purportedly "[fosters] what seems to be the ideal environment for the social solipsist," while podcasts represent "the opposite of radio" (Pitt 161; Arnold 207). Increasingly then, new audio-media usage is read as a willful self-exclusion from others, particularly in youth cultures (Collins). "Community-radio" podcast *Welcome to Night Vale* (*WTNV*) challenges such readings, often being used by its young fan-base not as an imaginative retreat to a "private utopia," but rather to a location, media form, and identity that are consciously and enthusiastically collective, frequently nostalgic and traditional, and purposefully shared (Bull 161).

This chapter argues *WTNV* fans build and experience community through imagined and performed "Night Vale" residence and community radio listenership, collective visual construction and definition of *WTNV*'s invisible spaces and inhabitants, and communication and collectivism enacted both as "cyber" and physically co-present audiences. In these aspects, *WTNV* suggests fresh potential for new audio-media and exposes alternate desires in audio-media users, as with each "broadcast" fan continue to cultivate old modes of community in new ways.

A Small Town That Intrigues and Comforts Us

"Night Vale" is a town where anybody can find community. That this ethos underpins *WTNV*'s identity is highlighted in co-creator Jeffrey Cranor's discussion of the show's second episode, which introduces a terrifying, mysterious Glow Cloud to the town: "I knew the moment we posted the episode what the Glow Cloud wanted because I knew then what *Night Vale* was. The Glow Cloud wanted what any of us wanted: to settle down in a small town that intrigues and comforts us" (Fink and Cranor, *Mostly Void, Partially Stars* 11). The Glow Cloud eventually joins the local Parent Teacher Association, becoming an integrated (albeit still tyrannical) member of the town's community. In this domestication of the strange, and in its articulation of such domestication through podcasting's "comforting analogue roots," *WTNV* achieves definition (Levy 1). Indeed, while *WTNV* is commonly, albeit loosely, ascribed "uncanny" tendencies whereby the familiar, homely, or *heimlich* (such as community radio) is made strange, of equal significance is the extent to which *WTNV* subverts this sensation, making the strange or unsettling familiar and known.[1]

"I KIND OF WANT TO LIVE IN NIGHT VALE"

The inclusion/domestication of non-normative persons within *WTNV*'s social fabric resonates strongly with fans. Discussing the podcast's success, Cecil Baldwin (who voices Cecil) states that "[h]umans love a good story ... especially one in which they can recognise themselves," and, while the show portrays a diverse, "representative" human population, *WTNV*'s monsters and "freaks" hold equal significance with the fan base (Butcher). Interviewing *WTNV* fans, Clint Nowicke reports, "Jenna from North Carolina identifies most with Carlos due to feeling like an outsider who finds a home in a strange environment. Hanna from Finland enjoys stories involving [severed hand and Night Vale elementary student] Megan Wallaby ... since they've shared similar feelings of loneliness and isolation." Likewise, explaining her life in "real" society, blogger thequintessentialqueer explicitly compares herself to *WTNV*'s non-human citizens: "we are made to feel monstrous. As a queer, autistic woman of colour, I have been taught to feel ugly, to feel dangerous, to feel dirty and wrong. In the absence of representation, I was spectral ... I am many headed and dangerous; I am faceless and afraid." Through *WTNV*'s diverse human representation, and the town's inclusion and acceptance of its ghosts, many-headed dragons, and faceless old woman, thequintessentialqueer's own "monstrosity" or *unheimlich* is made, literally, *heimlich*: "I am so grateful to Night Vale for being my strange, frightening, absurd home."

Repeatedly, *WTNV*'s hominess eclipses that of listeners' reality. Exploring Polish *WTNV* listenerships, Wlodarczyk and Tyminska report one listener "noted that when he listens to the podcast now, he feels as if he 'was going back home (however sappy that sounds)'" (4.6). Blogger solar_eclipse_eyes believes *WTNV*'s community creates "a sense of wish fulfillment, particularly for those who are hidden and unacceptable, and for those who are otherwise lost in the divide." Thequintessentialqueer presents *WTNV*'s horror as a matter of perspective: "fans would often describe Welcome to Night Vale as a horror podcast. I could never understand that ... Those who are trans, who are dark-skinned, who are disabled visibly or otherwise ... of course we love Night Vale. Of course [they] saw horror where we saw home." One reddit.com forum thread, asking whether listeners felt "prepared" by *WTNV* for real-world political events, generated a response deeming "Night Vale" more desirable than the real world—a sentiment encompassed in one response: "I don't know about feeling more prepared, but after I binge a bunch of episodes I want to drive through the desert searching. I kind of want to live in Night Vale" (self.nightvale). For many *WTNV* listeners, the town's strangeness constitutes not an unsettling horror environment but the comforting semblance of a wished-for home.

In domesticating the strange/Othered within a world of oddly traditionalistic, white-picket-fence, and apple-pie Americana, *WTNV* offers its listenership "[a] place where the community of a small town and a world tolerant of diversity intersect" (thoughtlessthinkythoughts). Traditional American community is re-imagined and revived as a space more socially connected, inclusive, and friendly than the reality beyond the earbuds, or as thoughtlessthinkythoughts puts it, "either way, I'd be living in a world filled with unspeakable horrors. I might as well choose the place that's honest about it. I might as well choose the place that would let me be my weird, quirky self. I might as well choose Night Vale."

That listeners find escape and hominess within *WTNV*/Night Vale contrasts starkly with the antisocial, individualistic tendencies attributed to new audio-media cultures. Yet such aspects are interrelated with the podcast's privatizing functions, allowing listeners not only "escape" but also immersion and intimacy, wherever and whenever they may be. Indeed, while solar_eclipse_eyes argues that *WTNV*'s "weird town" setting, "like Gravity Falls, like Eureka, [provides] a picture of a community where weirdness is out in the open and, somehow, normalized." *WTNV*'s appropriation of a community radio form enables a deeper facet of "wish fulfillment" than its televisual counterparts.[2]

While televisual "weird towns" may represent the inclusion and normalization of "strange" citizens, such communities exist at a necessary remove from the audience. The viewer is an extra-diegetic outsider, literally looking in; they may be "represented," but they are not actively included in the town and cannot enter the wished-for community. *WTNV* works differently. Audio is inherently more immersive than purely visually based media. It surrounds us, and coerces imaginative and highly personalized engagement, "making mass media and consciousness seem coextensive" (Verma 6). Through this, *WTNV*'s community radio identity offers stabilizing rhythm and locality. Solar_eclipse_eyes explains: "Our lives are so random. The world makes so little sense ... And then community radio comes along to give a narrative to the whole business; and, through narrative, the radio gives meaning." Yet there is hominess and safety to new audio-media's sound bubble. Discussing the potentials of headphone/earbud culture, Michael Collins observes,

> Sound and new technologies of sound distribution like the iPod have a special relationship to the experience of living, contentedly, within one's own, privatised universe. Indeed, of all the senses sound has perhaps the most to offer in terms of a subjective experience of homeliness, especially in an alien or alienating environment. Unlike the visual world, sound seems to own us and we to exist within it.

When paired with *WTNV*'s domestic community radio guise, new audio-media potentializes a mobile domestic, one in which the listener is not excluded but enveloped.

This sense of integration intensifies through Cecil's address and implication of the listener as a Night Vale citizen. Through feigning liveness and shared locality with his listeners, who are commonly addressed as "people of Night Vale" and "dear listeners of Night Vale," "the podcast listener's actual isolation from Night Vale and one another lessens: 'actual' differences in time and space are negated in the shared imaginary time and space of the broadcast. However, whenever and wherever listeners tune in from, they are tuning into the same reality" (Hancock 222). Moreover, the podcast's invisibility enables Night Vale's physicality to reside and develop within listeners' minds. Alexandra Brown notes that while "Night Vale's" architecture is "central to the narrative structure of the show ... [*WTNV*] avoids detailed descriptions of the town's architecture, with key buildings within Night Vale and its surrounds instead used as a series of recurring landmarks." In this sense, "Night Vale" as a cityscape and habitation of this space is not physically geographic but rather emotional or remembered—through individual engagement with the unfurling narrative.

Night Vale seems to fluctuate spatially, its boundaries shifting with events and individual interpretation. "Despite consistent references to Night Vale as a bustling or even quiet little town, as well as locations 'at the edge' or 'outside of' town, the size and—by extension—limits of Night Vale are deliberately unclear"; thus, "Night Vale is both a small town and an infinite city—a polemic rendered absolute by the medium of podcast" (Brown). Furthermore, Night Vale often appears to permeate the "real world": airplanes and trains from "real" cities "crash-land" there, invisible goods are claimed as the city's largest export, familiar "real-world" brands and companies exist there in slightly skewed form. Cecil appears telepathic and able to scry listeners' thoughts. Indeed, the recognition of "non-corporeal," silent, yet present and listening citizens suggests the invisible, unspeaking podcast listenership to be a known and accepted part of Night Vale's community (Fink and Cranor, "The Investigators"). Night Vale expands to encompass every auditor, in every time and space, and invites each "listener of Night Vale" to identify as a citizen.

"I'll Meet You at Arby's": Sharing "Night Vale"

Beyond expressing individual desires to "live" in "Night Vale," *WTNV* fans also seek to share, expand, and experience *WTNV*/Night Vale as a community. For many *WTNV* fans, the fact that Night Vale is a *shared* imaginative space rather than a "private utopia" is paramount to their engagement with the show. This is demonstrated through collective visual definition of the town space and inhabitants in the forms of online, collaborative "Night Vale community" role-play and fanfic, and the self-motivated formation of a collective listenership.

In terms of its popularity and sustained development, *WTNV* has always been affiliated with online community and cyber fandom. Independent podcasting relies on word-of-mouth or fellow-podcast endorsement for advertisement and, in *WTNV*'s history, fans' potency as a collective force is paramount as Cranor sources the show's sudden, immense, popularity to Tumblr: "Night Vale was everywhere on Tumblr. Fan art. Fan fiction. Slash fiction. Arguments over canon" (Fink and Cranor, *Mostly Void, Partially Stars* XIV). Alongside exposing fans' role in *WTNV*'s now-global notoriety, Cranor's comments further identify the extent to which fans have, from the start, collectively "claimed" and expanded *WTNV* beyond its podcast nexus.

Tumblr fandom gave *WTNV* a visual identity. Though *WTNV* exerts some visual identity through its logo, specific details concerning character and town appearance are not visually supplied and are seldom suggested within the audio narrative. Yet, as A observes, "there is a surprising alignment in visions of what Cecil Baldwin and his love interest, Carlos the scientist, look like." Cecil especially has found recognizable form as "the skinny, blond, bespectacled white guy with purple eye-shaped tattoos on his face and arms, who shows up with a simple Google search for Night Vale or Cecil Gershwin Palmer" (Okay_sure_lets_post). This image, generally sourced to Tumblr, has spread through the fandom to dominate both fan art and cosplay. Margaret Chwat, a popular *WTNV* fan-art creator, argues fan collaboration to underpin *WTNV* fan art's appeal as "people want to see images from what they can't actually see and build off what others have imagined" (qtd. in Carlson). Chwat suggests an almost hive-mind operation in the formation of synchronous imagery as "things that are weirdly, unconsciously the same" (qtd. in Carlson). Fans repeatedly attribute group sensibility to Cecil's visualization. Responding to Okay_sure_lets_post's reddit, one listener notes, "the fandom's understanding of him has changed over the years"; another fan observes that "the Cecils slowly evolve as new episodes come out and people continue to pass fanart around. Notice how many Cecils of color exist now? Some versions have remained nearly the same as they were in 2013 and have simply taken on a darker skin tone" (comment Okay_sure_lets_post), suggesting that the fandom's changing social consciousness is both influenced by, and influential of, Cecil's visual identity. Okay_sure_lets_post responds, "I actually imagined him with brown hair. But after seeing all these fan art depictions, my imagination has been supplanted by them." Through fan interaction and collaborative creativity, an invisible man finds form.

The extent to which fan community defines Cecil both unites and disrupts *WTNV* fandom. Some fans argue headcanon trends to privilege Caucasian race, male gender, and able-bodiedness, and in doing so disrupt open reading of such attributes. Others believe this stance to deny individual creativity or engagement with the show. However, many fans seek to rectify such misalignment within their "community." In a popular discussion of the fandom's fragmentation, *WTNV* blogger anightvaleintern posits problematics of representation as arising directly from the fandom's operation as a social grouping, and the responsibilities attendant to shared social environment. Posing the question "But what my headcanon is has no effect whatsoever on PoC's!" anightvaleintern responds, "Your individual headcanon has no effect on ... anything whatsoever. But in a group, it, once again, proves that people default to white. Which does effect PoC representation in the media and media representation is very important."

WTNV Blogger anightvaleintern further argues the issue to "open a dialogue" and asks fans to "use this as a rare chance to teach about expanding [racial and gendered] ideas." In such interactions, *Night Vale* fandom extends beyond the parameters of shared appreciation/discussion of the program and toward a meaningful social community, negotiating its own disputes and developing its own social contracts.

Less contentiously, the town's space is frequently defined and shared by online fans. Individual "outlining" and cooperative development of town maps, visual representation and familiarization of previously invisible buildings and spaces, and even one fan's (very popular) offer to "make you a desktop of your hometown as Night Vale or Desert Bluffs," exhibit the extent to which *WTNV* fandom increasingly, collectively identifies with the people *and* space of *WTNV* (npatchett).

Both *WTNV*'s reddit.com fan forum and comments sections of the show's numerous streaming sites further demonstrate fans building and sharing Night Vale identities and space. *WTNV*'s reddit.com page signals the extent to which the group's discussion revolves around shared, imaginative Night Vale habitation, through playful alteration of the show's Wikipedia description: "'Welcome to Night Vale is a podcast presented as a radio show for the ~~fictional~~ town of Night Vale, reporting on the strange events that occur within it.' –Wikipedia." Within the group, fans' usernames reflect their chosen identity within the town. Group moderators are referred to as members of "the Sheriff's Secret Police," teasingly reflecting their status as unseeable and somewhat omnipotent controllers. Other group members align themselves as "Night Valers" through affixing a *WTNV* identity to their username, including: "Librarian," "Hooded Figure," "you know, the farmer," "Desert Flower Bowling alley and aRcade fun complex employee," and "Eternal Scout."

Conversation within *WTNV*'s reddit forum and episode comment threads typically veers between distanced, consciously extra-fictional discussion of the podcast, and lively re-enactment or appropriation of the world which it depicts. While some discussions exclusively approach *WTNV* as fiction, much of *WTNV* fans' collective interaction revolves around the adoption of Night Vale resident identities, and group discussion of "town" and "community" issues. Through collective performance of Night Vale habitation, fans create their own *WTNV* storylines, perspectives, and scenarios within the forum threads, which develop through comment response, generating a collaborative role-play fan fiction. Recently aired episodes often constitute the impetus and context of such "in-character" discussions, with fans approaching show-events from their adopted Night Vale resident perspective. Thus, report of mega-corporation StrexCorp's infiltration of Night Vale prompted listener plans to "TAKE DOWN STREX" and then visit "Night Vale's" Arby's diner together)(er Imperious Condescension.

One such collaborative fan-fic provokes enlightening discussion concerning the difficulty in discerning "in character" and "out of character" forum participation. Following a confused role-play interaction, circuitZero (Street Cleaner) posits, "I think this sub will benefit greatly from (out of character: OOC) tags, I was 'in character' there," prompting discussion of role-play's ubiquity within the forum:

> *The_New_Doctor (You)*:   I think it would be better for IC [in-character] tags, as I feel most posts and comments are made out of character. OOC tags are useful for role-playing subs, of which this is not.
> *quitesavvy (Intern)*:   Except it kind of it [*sic*]
> *The_New_Doctor (You)*:   No it's not, the listeners here just treat it like it is. (The_New_Doctor)

Such interaction demonstrates the extent to which *WTNV*'s reddit increasingly, organically embodies an almost innately role-playing venture.

Ultimately, most online fan discussion comprises of a blend of "real world" and Night Vale "resident" stances. Yet even discussion threads that begin by approaching their topic with a consciously extra-fictional stance are frequently derailed to comply with the Night Vale residence fiction, as in podbay.com's "Street Cleaning Day" comment stream. The first comment reading "Tom Milsom for the weather! Awesome!" is immediately appropriated into the Night Vale role-play, as Kayjee17 responds, "[f]orget Tom Milsom and run, run, forget everything and run because it's STREET CLEANING DAY!!!!" (Kayjee17). The following thread of replies and new comments expand on Kayjee17's premise: that all listeners to *WTNV* are residents of Night Vale, experiencing a shared reality wherein street cleaning brings "removal" of homes, belongings, and loved ones; reference to the weather's musical content is deemed irrelevant and unintelligible. For many fans, then, the pleasure in online interaction lies not in distanced, "real-world" discussion of *WTNV* as a show, but in shared imaginative habitation of Night Vale as a community space.

These interactions evidence *WTNV*'s audio culture as rooted not simply in individuated listening but also in subsequent collective discussion and role-play. This complicates dominant conceptions of new audio-media as isolating and fragmentary. While fans may "tune-in" individually, from different places and temporalities, their online behaviors represent a more traditional understanding of audience than new audio-culture usually provokes, as fans form collective audience after the individuated listening experience. Thus we may argue, alongside Frances Gray's discussion of traditional radio audience, that "radio" audience is a collective which always, only exists after the broadcast, and is formed in the interactions which follow the necessarily individual listening event.[3] Much as, for Gray, listening is always solitary, and radio "arguably achieved true collective response when discussed the next day in the workplace, or when the catch-phrases or distinctive voices passed into common currency," we may deem *WTNV* fans' (perhaps) isolated listening situation as irrelevant: In their comments and threads we find the self-motivated formation of collective audience (232).

"The One Night We Could Take Off the Costume and Be Ourselves … Citizens of Night Vale"

Subversion of dominant, antisocial notions of new audio-culture culminates in *WTNV*'s live, theatrical shows. Herein emerges an extremely social, connective, and collaborative audio culture borne of previously disparate podcast listeners' desire to commune, not only imaginatively and via online forum, but physically.

Increasingly, *WTNV* live shows are typified by audience cosplay and, in being so, represent a highly visual, physically manifested realization of the town's previously imagined or online community. One fan's disappointment on attending an uncharacteristically low-costumed show illuminates the extent to which live shows represent a rare means for fans to physically embody the collective township of *WTNV*: "My only complaint was there were just not many cosplayers. Those who did, were great though. Of course, in a way, weren't we all cosplaying? As regular people? Or, was that the one night we could take off the costume and be ourselves. … Citizens of Night Vale" (Townsend). The connectivity that costume affords the podcast's previously disconnected, fragmented listenership has been noted: "[W]hen dressed as [*WTNV*] characters, fans are no longer strangers to one another; they become known and accessible through their costumes' inferred identity, and may relate to one another on this level" (Hancock 230). Yet the extent to which *WTNV*'s live shows are themselves focused on cultivating fan community and temporary embodiment of the otherwise imagined/online *WTNV* community remains undiscussed.

WTNV live shows operate around acknowledging and cultivating collective audience identity and interaction, both as *WTNV*'s "residents" and as a "real-world" community. During live shows, Cecil's "broadcast" generally reports that Night Vale residents have gathered in a large auditorium space. The rationale behind this town gathering varies, but always serves a common purpose: allowing the in-house audience to identify themselves as Cecil's intended listeners, the residents of Night Vale. Indeed, during "The Investigators," audiences are imaginatively situated alongside canonical town residents as Cecil's narrative places such figures among the gathering (Fink and Cranor, "The Investigators"). Beyond presenting the audience as the collective embodiment of *WTNV*'s community, live shows maneuver fans toward personal interaction through call and response sets. In "The Investigators," having explained that a murderer is loose, and that Night Vale's residents have assembled in the Rec center, Cecil describes the townspeople's actions. This guides the audience through a series of interpersonal engagements. These interactions begin with establishing and maintaining eye contact with a fellow "townsperson," and develop toward speaking with that person, co-enacting Cecil's humorously complicated physical direction, and eventually "solving" the murder mystery together.

Specifically, Cecil orchestrates engagement between strangers, explaining, "they looked past those people that they came with, or people who they might already know" (Fink and Cranor, "The Investigators"). This point is reiterated as, pre-empting the likely desire to "buddy-up" with a friend, Cecil interrupts the audience's initial actions, saying "No no no no. They sought out the eyes of a complete stranger." Disengagement with role-play sections is further admonished, and afforded rectification, as Cecil later explains that "those people who just refused to look around them, and so now found themselves without a partner ... took this opportunity to jump on board, and so they found somebody else that was similarly reluctant to participate." As the directed role-play continues, its narrative moves the audience pairs through initial stages of their characters' distrust, grudging cooperation, and eventual collaborative success as "ex-strangers ... friends," mirroring and highlighting the stages by which these "actors" have become acquainted.

As "The Investigators" concludes, the role-play spell is gently broken; "the evening turns to night. And soon, all of the citizens of Night Vale will disperse back to their homes." *WTNV*'s briefly embodied community is splintered, transformed back to strangers, with different towns to return to, and only imagined and online acts of citizenship to bind them. Yet Cecil urges his audience to retain its sentiment of community, out in the "real world":

[F]or this one evening, we all came together. And what are human beings but a coming together? What are we for, except to lean into those around us, to balance against those around us. A delicate but provocative sculpture…

Look, harm can come from anywhere, or anyone. Whether it is a stranger, or a friend. But still, we reach out the hand. Still, we allow our eyes to meet. Still, we hope for the best, and we try to be the best in return because if not, then what else? If not, then nothing. A human life, it's just this. It's a moment of eye contact in a crowd.

Collectivity defines the live *WTNV* experience; the shows enable previously dispersed podcast listeners both to listen together *and* to create and enact a true listening community. As reviewer Ciaran notes, "The Night Vale live shows are really a community event; you may not know anybody, but you're all here for the same reason. You all share the same energy in the same space. And really, isn't that truly what community is all about?"

CONCLUSION

WTNV offers an alternate perspective on new audio-media, suggesting that within its young fan-base there is desire to escape not from community, but toward it. Community and collectivism represent key features of fan interaction and engagement with *WTNV*, with fans increasingly embracing and developing the show's fantasy of shared location, listenership, and identity. As Nowicke observes, *WTNV* "is more than just a podcast full of supernatural oddities, it's a community" (Nowicke). Indeed, beyond enabling fictional community, *WTNV* frequently appears to encourage extra-diegetic collectivism as "[Cecil] sells us the concept of activism and community participation" (sigmalibrae). *WTNV* listeners do not represent "anti-social beings, those who avoid human interaction," nor does the podcast exist as a means to "reverse the modern intent of the concert hall or public address system as means of organising a collective 'culture of listening'" (Pitt 161; Tonkiss qtd. in Collins). Rather, through its podcast, online and on-stage incarnations, *WTNV* has, as Butcher puts it, "created a community."

NOTES

1. This subverted uncanny is often overt. Ghosts, doubles, and automatons, all figures charged with *unheimlich* potential, find home and community within Night Vale. Likewise, while severed hands have "something peculiarly uncanny about them, especially when … able to move of themselves," in

WTNV, detached hand "Megan Wallaby" is given voice, name, family, and a community which cares deeply for her need for social integration (Freud 14).

2. *Gravity Falls* (2012–2016) is a Disney Channel cartoon series detailing the mysterious and often supernatural happenings of the eponymous Gravity Falls, a strange rural town. Likewise, *Eureka* (2006–2012) explores the scientific oddities and conspiracies of the research community Eureka, Oregon.

3. Indeed, radio scholarship broadly acknowledges the extent to which traditional radio forged an illusion rather than actuality of community/collective identity between its listeners, as much dependent upon the medium's cultivated modes of address and content as its liveness.

Works Cited

"A. 10 Reasons to Listen to Welcome to Night Vale." *The Artifice*. www.the-artifice.com/welcome-to-night-vale/.

Anightvaleintern. "Maggie's Comprehensive Guide to Cecil Headcanons with Regards to Racism." *Tumblr*. www.anightvaleintern.tumblr.com/post/58629211053/maggies-comprehensive-guide-to-cecil-headcanons.

Arnold, Regina. "Podcrastination." In *iPod and Philosophy: iCon of an ePoch*, ed. D.E. Wittkower, 205–214. Chicago, IL: Open Court Publishing, 2008.

Brown, Alexandra. "The Continuous Monument and the Brown Stone Spire: Radicality in the Architecture of Night Vale." *Architechturetemps*. www.architecturemps.com/wp-content/uploads/2013/09/BROWN-ALEXANDRA_THE-CONTINUOUS-MONUMENT-AND-THE-BROWN-STONE-SPIRE_NIGHT-VALE.pdf.

Butcher, Ryan. "Welcome to Night Vale's Cecil Baldwin: 'Young People Use Night Vale to Begin the Conversation about Their Own Sexuality.'" *Gaytimes*. www.gaytimes.co.uk/culture/9151/welcome-to-night-vales-cecil-baldwin-young-people-use-night-vale-to-begin-the-conversation-about-their-own-sexuality/.

Bull, Michael. *Sound Moves*. New York: Routledge, 2007.

Carlson, Adam. "America's Most Popular Podcast: What the Internet Did to Welcome to Night Vale." *Theawl*. www.theawl.com/americas-most-popular-podcast-what-the-internet-did-to-welcome-to-night-vale-ba78f910fe2#.6rg3fpgpn.

Ciaran. "Review: Night Vale Live Show: The Investigators." *Geekireland*. www.geekireland.com/review-night-vale-live-show-investigators/.

Collins, Michael J. "Pod People: Brave New Worlds of Digital Audio Drama." *Alluvium* 5, no. 4 (2016). Accessed February 14, 2017. https://doi.org/10.7766/alluvium.v5.4.01.

Fink, Joseph, and Jeffrey Cranor. *The Great Glowing Coils of the Universe: Welcome to Night Vale Episodes, Volume 2*. London: Orbit, 2016a.

———. "The Investigators: Live." *Bandcamp*. www.nightvale.bandcamp.com/album/the-investigators-live.

———. *Mostly Void, Partially Stars: Welcome to Night Vale Episodes Volume 1.* London: Orbit, 2016b.

Freud, Sigmund. *The Uncanny.* London: Penguin, 2003.

Gray, Frances. "Fireside Issues: Audience, Listener, Soundscape." In *More Than a Music Box*, ed. Andrew Crisell, 247–264. New York, London: Berghahn, 2003.

Hand, Richard, and Mary Traynor. *The Radio Drama Handbook.* New York, NY: Continuum, 2011.

Kayjee17. "Re: Street Cleaning Day." *Podbay.* www.podbay.fm/show/536258179/e/1358254800?autostart=1.

Lacey, Kate. "Listening in the Digital Age." In *Radio's New Wave: Global Sound in the Digital Age*, ed. Jason Loviglio and Michele Hilmes, 9–23. Abingdon: Routledge, 2013.

Levy, Steven. *The Perfect Thing.* London: Ebury Press, 2006.

Nowicke, Clint. "The Welcome to Night Vale Community: Where No One Is Wrong and Everyone Is Allowed to Be Unique." *Popmythology.* www.popmythology.com/welcome-to-night-vale-where-no-one-is-wrong-and-everyone-is-allowed-to-be-unique/.

Npatchett. "Will Make You a Desktop of Your Hometown as Night Vale or Desert Bluffs." *Reddit.* www.reddit.com/r/nightvale/comments/3jcd88/will_make_you_a_desktop_of_your_hometown_as_night/.

Okay_sure_lets_post. "Where Did the Common Visual Depiction of Cecil Arise?" *Reddit.* www.reddit.com/r/nightvale/comments/2hlife/where_did_the_common_visual_depiction_of_cecil/.

Pitt, Joseph C. "Don't Talk to Me." In *iPod and Philosophy: iCon of an ePoch*, ed. D.E. Wittkower, 161–168. Chicago, IL: Open Court Publishing, 2008.

self.nightvale. "Does Anyone Else Feel Slightly More Prepared for the Worlds Current Political Climate After Listening to WTNV?" *Reddit.* www.reddit.com/r/nightvale/comments/5qug1h/does_anyone_else_feel_slightly_more_prepared_for/.

Sigmalibrae. "How Do I Love Thee?" *Tumblr.* www.sigmalibrae.tumblr.com/post/81468358728/how-do-i-love-thee-let-me-count-the-ways-an.

Solar_eclipse_eyes. "WTNV Reflections and Nocturnes." *Tumblr.* www.solar-eclipse-eyes.tumblr.com.

Thequintessentialqueer. "A Singularity in Blue." *Tumblr.* www.thequintessentialqueer.tumblr.com/post/145948852858/there-are-no-words-in-me-with-which-to-express-how.

The_New_Doctor. "How One Finds Night Vale's Radio Station?" *Reddit.* www.reddit.com/r/nightvale/comments/43u3nn/how_one_finds_night_vales_radio_station/.

Thoughtlessthinkythoughts. "Deep Thoughts Except When Not." *Tumblr.* www.thoughtlessthinkythoughts.tumblr.com/post/79954447823/creepy-cuttingedge-and-cecilos-litbythestars.

Townsend, Alex. "See the Horror You Can Only Hear! The Night Vale Live Show Experience." *Themarysue*. www.themarysue.com/night-vale-live-experience/.

Verma, Neil. *Theater of the Mind: Imagination, Aesthetics and American Radio Drama*. Chicago, IL: University of Chicago Press, 2012.

Wlodarczyk, Agata, and Marta Tyminska. "Cultural Differences: Polish Fandom of Welcome to Night Vale." *Transformative Works and Cultures* no. 19 (2015). Accessed February 14, 2017. https://doi.org/10.3983/twc.2015.0591.

)(er Imperious Condescension. "Re: Old Oak Doors Part B." *Podbay*. www.podbay.fm/show/536258179/e/1404187200?autostart=1#comment-1463447237.

CHAPTER 4

On Floating Cats, Good Boys, and Shapeshifting Zookeepers: Animals in *Night Vale*

Heidi Lyn

Abstract Night Vale is full of conspiracies, scientists, monsters, gods, and the people who live in the tiny city under lane 5 of the Desert Flower Bowling Alley and Arcade Fun Complex. However, the city is also full of more familiar animals like deer, dogs, cats, and zoo animals. As is typical of Night Vale, much of the time these animals are strangely different than those we know. They may have spines, venom sacs, or float four feet above the ground. But other times, despite their weirdness, they are presented in such a way that they conform to the attitudes and prejudices that animal scientists are all too familiar with. As one of these animal scientists, I will take a look at the furred and clawed denizens of Night Vale and pick apart the weird, the not-so-weird, and the downright normal in their characters.

Keywords Animals • Cats • Dogs • Science • Zoo

H. Lyn (✉)
The University of South Alabama, Mobile, AL, USA
e-mail: Heidi.Lyn@usm.edu

© The Author(s) 2018
J. A. Weinstock (ed.), *Critical Approaches to* Welcome to Night Vale,
https://doi.org/10.1007/978-3-319-93091-6_4

INTRODUCTION FROM THE AUTHOR

I am a scientist. Not like Carlos is a scientist. I don't pour colorful liquids into and out of bubbling beakers, nor do I wear a lab coat. On the other hand, like Carlos, I'm a Taurus and I've been thinking about getting a tattoo with the definition of Science—right out of Webster's Dictionary: "I don't know, but I'm trying to find out, OK?" (episode 65, "Voicemail"). While Carlos doesn't study chemistry or biology (he studies "science"), I study animals, specifically, how animal minds are similar to or different from human minds. While he has spent much time saving Night Vale from infestations, attacks, and all manner of danger (although he reminds us that he is not a hero, just a scientist), I have not had to save anyone from anything quite so dramatic. Heroics aside, the study of real-world animals can nevertheless be dangerous—dangerous to one's state of cleanliness, to one's understanding of the world, and particularly to one's idea of human uniqueness.

Many people's ideas of human uniqueness center around language or, alternately, consciousness. These are some of the questions that I've spent my entire professional career exploring. Do animals possess the capacity for language? Do they have a sense of self? Can they count? Can they learn from each other? While investigating these questions, I've done some things and gained some personal experiences that may sound like the stuff of science fiction. I've had dolphins inform me of possible intruders into the lab space. I've had a bonobo tell me a story about a monster in the woods. I've played video games, both with dolphins on a five-foot television screen and with chimpanzees on computers using their own joysticks. I've looked in mirrors with walrus, seals, and belugas. What has consistently become clear through these personal experiences, but more importantly, through the research findings across the field, is that what we think is a definitive difference between us and them is a much blurrier line.[1]

ANIMALS IN NIGHT VALE

Night Vale is a fantastical place. *Welcome to Night Vale*, the podcast, thrives on taking what may be considered "weird" and treating it as normal and then taking it even a step further—pushing the boundaries of what we thought was weird by increasing that weirdness. We might assume that animals that are resident in such a town might be equally fantastical, equally weird—and there are certainly some examples of fantastical animals in town. However, all too frequently, the authors fall into well-established and typical attitudes when considering animals. In this chapter, I'll take a look at the extra weird and the, perhaps disappointingly, not-so-weird animals in this quiet little desert town, which I think helps to limn our own conventional understandings of what animals are and are not. *Night Vale* is often weird but on occasion—where animals are concerned—perhaps not weird enough.

When looking at the animals of Night Vale, I will be limiting my focus to animals that have the same names as those in the world we live in—for example, cats and dogs. That leaves out antiques (somewhere between animals and people), Librarians (somewhere between monsters and people), and plastic bags that are, at first, mistaken for dogs. In addition, animals that are completely mythological and can therefore not be studied in the real world will be left out (like certain five-headed dragons I could mention). Some of the animals I will cover gain some monstrous characteristics (most notably a range of spines and venom sacs), but remain animals—most notably by maintaining the inability to use human language.

Language in animals is a trickier question than has typically been presented in the science fiction/fantasy genre—where animals generally either have it or they don't. In multiple studies over close to 50 years now, researchers have found that different animal species have the capacity to use some parts of human language (see Lyn, "Apes and the Evolution of Language" for a review of 40 years' worth of animal language studies). Dolphins can understand complicated audio and gestural "sentences" and respond differentially depending on the syntactical structure (Herman, Pack, et al.; Herman, Kuczaj, et al.). Parrots can identify objects based on material, shape, and number (Pepperberg). Apes can use gestures (Gardner et al.; Patterson and Linden) and computer keyboards (Pate and Rumbaugh; Savage-Rumbaugh and Lewin) to communicate about objects and people.

More recent studies have shown that apes' use of symbols is not simple association and that the errors they make when choosing symbols closely parallel the errors made by humans when they speak (Lyn, "Mental Representation of Symbols"). Also, these symbol-using apes seem to be fundamentally changed in a way that brings them closer to humans (at least as far as our testing methods can measure). For example, symbol-using apes understand human body language like pointing better than apes that haven't had those experiences (Lyn, Russell, et al.) and they use much more complicated forms of pretend play (Lyn, Greenfield, et al.). Most apes "pretend"; they "eat" off of pictures of food, for example. But only the apes that were symbol competent would pick up a monster doll and chase their caretakers with it, or pull an imaginary pull toy—even pretending to yank it free after it got "stuck" (Kellogg and Kellogg; Lyn, Greenfield, et al.). These behaviors might sound fantastical or simply over-interpreted, but time and again, our tests of animals' thoughts and abilities show that they are capable of more than we assume.

Talking animals (animals with language) are a mainstay in fantasy and even in science fiction (McKechnie and Miller; Vint). Several works even specifically discuss the distinctions between animals without language and those with it (often termed Talking Animals, *amborgs* [Gordon, "Learning to Live With the Animals in SF"], or simply Animals with a capital A). For example, Talking Animals in the *Narnia* series are descended from pairs specifically chosen by Aslan, the lion deity of that world, and the treatment of these Talking Animals underscores the clear Christian allegorical themes of the *Narnia* books. They are larger than regular animals and have an intellect on par with humans, serving, in effect, as stand-ins for humans—God's chosen. Similar to the creation story of the Christian Bible, when the Talking Animals are first created, Aslan gives them dominion over the dumb animals, but warns them not to "go back to their ways lest you cease to be Talking Beasts" (*Magician's Nephew* 92), seemingly a metaphor for the potential human loss of religion and grace.

In the *Wicked Years* books by Gregory Maguire, Animals (with a capital letter) are shunned because they are too similar to humans—witness the persecution and probable murder of Dr. Dillamond, the Goat professor. Dr. Dillamond had been trying to prove the equivalence of humans and Animals as a bid to eliminate the new laws making discrimination against Animals legal. After his death and the failure of the Animals' movement, persecuted Animals seek out and return to the society of animals and, as they no longer speak and exercise the traits associated with their sentience, they cease to be Animals (competition for humans) and become animals (companions for humans). This kind of discomfort with Talking Animals is seen in many other science fiction and fantasy stories. As Johnson says, "[T]hey all could frame their thoughts well enough to talk. ... And we found that, really, we prefer our slaves mute" (277).

Language, therefore, is not just a method of communication; it serves as a perceived dividing line between what is animal and what is human, or even divine (Gordon, "Talking (For, with) Dogs: Science Fiction Breaks a Species Barrier" 457). *Night Vale*, however, like it does with many other beliefs, tends to simply ignore that line. Science fiction is often at its most influential when it challenges cultural convention and presents a potential future that is frightening (e.g., classic works by Orwell, Atwood, and Huxley that often seem all too accurate as predictors of the future). *Night Vale* is a prime example of this type of science fiction that foregrounds, challenges, and contradicts the attitudes and mores of the time—for example, sexual orientation (see Stobbart, this volume). *Night Vale* ignores the considerable topical interest of homosexuality and presents the love affair between Cecil and Carlos as a romance, with no reference to their sexuality at all. In the case of Cecil and Carlos, this can be seen as a statement in and of itself. The sexuality of a romantic partnership is seen as irrelevant to a large and growing part of the population; therefore, by ignoring the issue, the authors of *Welcome to Night Vale* align themselves with that emerging point of view.

Similarly, when it comes to animals, some animals can talk, some can't. Neither is remarked upon. Rabbits invade a fundraising headquarters and, as a listener begins to picture little bunnies chewing on phone wires, they are instead informed that the rabbits were "using dedicated telephone lines to make personal calls, uttering insensitive remarks about the body types of students and staff, and tilting the vending machines in clear violation of safety labeling" (episode 50, "Capital Campaign"). This utter dismissal of a fundamental perception that is rooted in our cultural landscape is typical of *Welcome to Night Vale*.

One of the first animals we meet in *Night Vale* (other than all those dogs that are not allowed in the Dog Park) is Khoshekh, the cat that occupies a fixed point hovering four feet above the ground in the men's bathroom of the radio station. *Night Vale*'s attitude toward Khoshekh and its other animal denizens was summarized very neatly at the end of episode 111 ("Summer 2017, Night Vale, USA"). In it, Carlos had been reacquainting himself with the weirdness of Night Vale. He believes he has grown too used to the town it to see the weirdness with clear eyes. During a lunch break, Cecil and Carlos go to the men's bathroom to feed and pet Khoshekh.

> *Cecil*: Carlos pointed out cats don't float. I stared at Khoshekh, having never really thought about that. After a bit I said, "This one does."
> Carlos smiled, petted Khoshekh between the eyes and went back to his work, and I went back to mine.

When listeners ask for photographs of Khoshekh, we are reminded that life is often disposable in Night Vale. Cecil demurs on the photo requests by reminding listeners that radio is not a visual medium, while also mentioning that the few individuals who had tried to take photos of the cat died ago-nizing deaths within a week, so no photos for now. Those deaths—and the deaths of almost every intern to work in the radio station—are mentioned briefly and then almost forgotten. Animal life is equally disposable—indeed, when Khoshekh arrives in the station Cecil mentions that Makayla, who works in sales, so enjoyed having a cat she put her Weimaraner to sleep and adopted a litter of tabby kittens (episode 9, "Pyramid").

This disregard for the world with which we are most familiar is echoed by *Night Vale*'s presentation of several animal species. Deer are the perfect example. In Night Vale, deer are often struck by cars. Of course, deer are struck by cars in the world we know; however, in Night Vale, this is a pur-poseful action by the deer (who are all named Deer) because they have mastered the art of short-distance time travel—when they are hit by a car, they travel back in time to before they were hit. Their momentary pain and disorientation is simply the price they pay for that experience. Also, (just another characteristic of Deer) if you want to purchase a house, you must first stab a deer through the chest to release the Real Estate Agent that lives inside. This sideways look at the world that we know is a staple of the *Night Vale* universe.

In contrast, some of the treatment of animals in town echoes the well-established, albeit contradictory nature of humanity's attitude and expec-tations toward the animals that share our world. Every day, we have to manage the cognitive dissonance surrounding our relationships with ani-mals. We see and hear stories of animal mistreatment to the tune of Sarah McLachlan's "In the Arms of the Angel" juxtaposed with the cute kitten pics that make up a large part of the internet. We read countless stories about cats and dogs that are treated and treasured as family members and yet we also must make decisions about the food we ingest. We sometimes manage these contradictions by avoidance—most meat eaters prefer to divorce themselves from thoughts of their food when it was alive. Other methods of coping include dividing up animal species into "food ani-mals," "wild animals," and "pet animals"—among other categorizations (Herzog; King). In our culture, we balk at the very idea of eating cats and dogs, while across most of India, slaughtering cows is illegal as cattle are considered sacred by many Hindu practitioners. These contradictory thought processes are well known, with a growing number of researchers exploring the topic in a field dubbed anthrozoology or simply human-animal relations.

Due to the inherent cognitive dissonance of the relationships, humans regularly approach even their daily interactions with animals with determinedly flawed logic. For example, to maintain a belief in her vegetarianism, a woman argued well into adulthood that fish are not animals in the same way that, say, chickens are (Herzog). The confounding and confusing nature of human attitudes toward animals is well known to anyone that makes a study of animals (Herzog) and includes a range of preconceptions about animals' abilities, attitudes, and our own behaviors in relation to pets. In many ways, *Night Vale*, for all its wonderful weirdness, fails to break free of many of these pervading attitudes.

Even Cecil's attitude toward Khoshekh echoes some well-known prejudices regarding cats and dogs. Cecil mentions several times that he is not a "cat person," but he has come to love Khoshekh. This echoes many people's perceptions of cats as removed and standoffish, and our basic attitude toward "cat people." We actually have many stereotypes about people who prefer specific animals. For example, there is an automatic stereotype of people who keep pet snakes or spiders as odd or anti-social. Even more interesting, some of that stereotyping is borne out in personality studies. People who self-identify as dog people have been shown be more extroverted, socially dominant, and agreeable, and less neurotic and open than cat people (Gosling et al.; Alba and Haslam). Therefore, Cecil's declaration of love for Khoshekh is more important than simply admitting a fondness for a particular animal—to admit as a dog person that you love a cat is admitting to being a different type of person, potentially contradicting your former self-concept. Recall that when Makayla in sales became enamored of Khoshekh, she chose to put her dog to sleep and adopt a litter of kittens, underscoring the cultural belief that one has to choose between dogs and cats (episode 9, "Pyramid").

Another sometimes unacknowledged stereotype is the "gendering" of animal species—for example, dogs are more masculine, while cats are generally perceived as feminine, regardless of actual sex (Harrison; Nelson). This gendering extends to the perception of individuals, with the frequent bizarre consequence of having confused sexing of animals in many forms—for example, cartoon male "cows," complete with udders. Because of these pre-suppositions, most cats are immediately perceived as being female or at least having female traits (Harrison; Nelson). This gendered perception extends to their owners; for example, when two gay men were labeled as cat people, they were rated as less masculine than when labeled as dog people (Mitchell and Ellis). Khoshekh, in defiance of this tendency, but supporting the confused gendering of individuals, is male. Male pronouns are used exclusively, even when Khoshekh, without moving from his hovering location, spontaneously gives birth to a litter of kittens. In fact, Cecil dismisses the question of how a male cat could have babies as something that just shouldn't be questioned—like how a cat could be hovering in a fixed location in the first place.

It should be noted that, as Khoshekh's kittens get older, *Night Vale* explores another recurring theme, the twisting of physical form. Like deer, which have multiple forms (some two-headed, or spider-eyed, or four-armed and radioactive), the kittens have physical forms unlike their real-life counterparts, which on first blush, buoys the weirdness of *Night Vale*. The authors use these physical manifestations for multiple purposes. The most obvious is to inspire humor, which, by definition, requires a sudden undercutting of expectation (Martin). *Night Vale* follows this definition often, with Cecil's beginning innocuous descriptions that suddenly take a sharp turn. For example, when introducing the kittens:

> Oh! Some great news to all of you out there who adopted kittens from Khoshekh, the cat floating in our station bathroom. Well, it's been several months, and the kittens have just been growing like you wouldn't believe! They've molted twice, and some of them are already getting their grownup kitty spine ridges! (episode 39, "The Woman from Italy")

Other examples of this progressive distortion of reality include the StrexPet (episode 43, "Visitor") and the beagle puppy (multiple episodes, especially 89 and 90, "Who's a good boy?" parts 1 and 2). In both cases, the first reaction Cecil has is overwhelming appreciation of the cuteness. Only after a short period of time, does he begin to suspect that they may not, in fact, be so cute.

> Here boy! ... or girl! ... or either! Come get some water! Come here! You're so *cute! So so so so so cute!*
>
> Nope. Didn't move. But its eyes followed me as I moved in my chair. Or ... did they?
>
> They're just solid black, all pupil, like umm ... a what? A spider? Well that'd be weird. There are some other dark dots around its face. Could be eyes, but ... no, I don't think it's—ooh! Wait! That noise again! Listen!
>
> Oh! Well, whatever it is, it is *cuuute!* Or, weirdly cute! Or just weird. Ugh! Uh! OK. (episode 43, "Visitor")

He padded forwards. He was ... *adorable*! Or ... was he? I—I had thought he was a cute ... beagle puppy, but ... there was ... something ... *off* about him. A sneer in his lips, a—a—a strange bend to his legs, his—his body was misshapen. It—it—no, he was *not cute at all!* (episode 89, "Who's a Good Boy?" Part 1)

In these examples, the purpose of the altered perception is not to inspire humor, but rather a creeping sense that all is not right with these "animals" (the StrexPet eventually being revealed as a bio-mechanical object and the beagle puppy as the result of a summoning gone wrong). In both cases, too, part of the horror of the actions of the animals comes from the contrast with that first perception. Psychologically, however, this shift in attitude also serves to invoke a well-known—although again frequently unacknowledged—deep-seated discomfort that many people feel with animals, even their own pets. Because animals are perceived as "like us" but also not, we often misinterpret their behaviors and motivations as their natural tendencies butt up against some of our greatest prejudices and taboos.

While many people have come to treat pets like family members, this hasn't always been the case. In early days of domestication, animals were brought into homes because they had jobs. Cats were to manage vermin; horses were to assist with physical labor (either pulling or being ridden). Dogs had more varied jobs, including hunting assistance, guarding homes or flocks, or, in the case of many small dog species, bed/foot warmers (Serpell 7). As many of those jobs became less important, the natural attachment humans felt toward their pets became a more central part of the relationship. We can posit that, today, the majority of people feel their pets are fur-babies (even if they would never use that term); many carry them in their pocketbooks, dress them in clothing, and share pictures of them on social media thereby continuing the characterization of pets as mini-people. This is all fine and good until pets do something outside of that definition—until they act like (gasp!) animals.

This attitude shift usually surrounds activities that humans have relegated to private rooms: evacuation and mating (how embarrassing if one's cats spray urine and your house smells like a feline toilet, or if your dog tries to hump your boss's leg!). One modern way owners express this attitude conflict is with the phenomenon of pet-shaming. Pets are photographed with a sign that explains their transgression, which is then shared on social media. These transgressions often involve the activities mentioned above: eating, elimination, or mating behavior ("Dog Shaming"). Interestingly, although the websites are labeled as pet-shaming, shame is considered a second-order emotion—that is, an emotion that is defined by how you think others will perceive you. Animals have not been shown to display second-order behaviors of this kind, so pet-shaming is a clear example of humans placing their values and perceptions onto their pets (Lyn and Savage-Rumbaugh). The shame belongs to the owner, not the animal—although the owners seem to be attempting to shift said blame by a public declaration: "It's not our fault! Our pets are terrible, they are just horrible at acting like humans!"

This discomfort with animal behaviors in our pets is particularly strong when animals fight or bite. Aggression is one of the most frequent behaviors listed for owner surrenders to shelters (Alberthsen et al.). Aggressive behaviors are also almost never shared on pet-shaming sites. Seemingly, humans feel stronger levels of embarrassment or disgust with aggression than with other "shameful" behaviors. When animals show their animal side, particularly aggressive behaviors, we can no longer pretend that they are mini-humans. This often leads to a complete rejection as these "family members" have turned on us. The actions of two animals in *Night Vale*, the Beagle puppy and the StrexPet, tap into these uncomfortable feelings. The behavior of the StrexPet, in particular, illustrates our strong discomfort with aggression. In "Visitor," the StrexPet is introduced as a cute, unknown animal that has appeared at the radio station. Cecil initially referred to the StrexPet as "the little guy or gal" and tries to make friends—approaching and trying to pet it. The StrexPet then clutches his leg—still an adorable behavior—but then bites Cecil and continues to the men's room, where it attacks Khoshekh. Once Cecil realizes he's been bitten, the StrexPet immediately becomes "this *thing*," with any mention of its cuteness disappearing. Of course, once the StrexPet turns on the beloved Khoshekh, it is demoted even further: to monster.

Underscoring our discomfort with animal violence, the "Visitor" episode resulted in an extremely strong negative fan response. An example, and the most up-voted comment on the episode on podbay, is, "Alright this is where I draw the line! They've hurt my Cecil, they've hurt my Carlos, but when you HURT KHOSHEKH, MY BABY KITTY ... Let's just say I'm more than ready for this war!! MAKE 'EM BLEED!" (Unicorns-at-arbys). On many chat rooms, horror and disbelief were clearly in evidence, particularly as Khoshekh's life hung in the balance at the end of the episode. It is a noteworthy dichotomy: Khoshekh—who clearly displays otherworldly attributes including spines and venom sacs (if his kittens are any indication)—is a beloved member of the *Night Vale* universe and potential danger to him is mourned. The StrexPet, on the other hand, displays no dangerous physical characteristics, but has behaved unacceptably and is now reviled. The fan reaction also belies the previous conclusion about the nature of danger and death in *Night Vale* being contradictory in the extreme. The typical nonchalance surrounding the deaths of members of the Night Vale community does not extend to characters that are named and, more importantly, that behave well.

The authors of *Welcome to Night Vale* also capitalize on our unconscious stereotypes of cute animals as being good. The StrexPet and later the Beagle puppy are particularly impactful "villains" given their initial introductions. In the case of the beagle puppy, it's even a case of breed-based stereotyping. Consider this exchange between Cecil and former intern Maureen who has dropped by the station with her new puppy:

Cecil: That's a good question. Another good question is, "Who's a good boy? Who's a good boy!"

Maureen: This dog is, obviously! He's a beagle! Therefore, he's a good boy! (episode 81, "After 3327")

There are undeniable breed stereotypes, with many being beloved (e.g. Beagles, Dalmatians, Golden Retrievers) and others reviled by some (Dobermans, Rottweilers, Pit Bulls) (Serpell 65). Often these stereotypes are based not in reality, but on the media's coverage. For example, each time a *101 Dalmatians* movie has been released, the adoption and breeding rates of Dalmatians has soared, even though Dalmatians are not a breed that works well in all households. Similarly, in each generation, there is an "evil" dog breed. In the 1980s and 1990s, it was Doberman Pinschers and Rottweilers; in the twenty-first century, it's Pit Bulls that get ignored and left unadopted in shelters at staggering rates. There are campaigns from multiple animal welfare organizations attempting to change the public's perception of these breeds, but in many cases, the attitudes cannot be shifted easily. In Night Vale, the populace is more pragmatic; once the beagle puppy reveals his malevolent intentions, the humans organize mass resistance. It should be noted that the switch from adorable puppy to nightmarish monster trying to control all of Night Vale's citizens does not, of course, alter the puppy's perception of itself in any way.

"I am the good boy, Cecil!" the beagle said. "You ... wanted ... to ... witness. So ... witness! I ... am the good ... boy, and I rule ... over the dark ... wet caverns ... of ... Hellllllllllllllll!" (episode 92, "If He Had Lived")

Another subject in which *Night Vale* fails to break from the cultural *zeitgeist* is the keeping and protection of wild animals. This is also a topic that is plagued by illogical thinking, as are related issues including conservation efforts, human encroachment into wild environments, pollution, research, and zoos. Many people seem to have no difficulties accepting that animals in the wild are "free" and happy at the same time that they recognize (although often fail to mention) that these animals are endangered and beleaguered. For example, large animal rights groups have thrown their full weight behind the idea of shutting down captive displays of marine mammals and, therefore, necessarily releasing captive whales and dolphins back into the wild ("Marine Mammals in Captivity"; "Aquariums and Marine Parks"). They argue that marine parks are, in effect, prisons, and that animals in captivity live shorter lives than those in the wild, although many of these assertions do not hold up to scientific scrutiny (Robeck et al.). The documentaries and arguments that oppose marine parks often ignore or avoid discussing threats to these animals in the wild. For instance, one population of killer whales in the wild is declining at a very high rate ("NOAA Fisheries"). Researchers attempting to determine the reasons for the decline have found many possibilities including the decline of prey species, stress due to human interaction, and toxins. Is it better, therefore, given all of the data, to return an animal to a wild environment that not only is completely unfamiliar (as most orcas have been born in captivity) but is also dangerous?

Similarly, the Vancouver Aquarium recently announced that it will no longer keep captive dolphins or whales ("Friends of the Vancouver Aquarium"), which would shut down its rescue center for stranded marine mammals. In many cases, these stranded animals would not survive if returned to the wild, leading to a difficult choice: Do you return these animals to certain death in the wild, or euthanize them right on the beach? In the popular press and the cultural *zeitgeist*, the thorny nature of these issues is almost always ignored in favor of pat answers. Animals should not be imprisoned; the wild is always best; zoos and aquariums are evil.

The authors of *Night Vale*, in the episode appropriately titled "Zookeeper" (episode 95), fall squarely into that *zeitgeist*. In contrast to the domesticated animals that are the norm for *Night Vale*, here we get a glimpse of the oft-mentioned but never visited Night Vale Zoo in the form of a visit from head zookeeper, Joanna Rey. Joanna does spend some time explaining her animals and the development programs of the zoo, but also apparently absent-mindedly agrees with Cecil's characterization of the zoo as a prison.

> *Cecil:* Is there any consideration by the zoo about developing sentience in creatures who live in cages? I mean, do you think that the animals' self-awareness could bring about stages of depression or resentment, or despair or even rage, if they understood the prison-like conditions in which they lived?
>
> *Joanna:* Totally. (episode 95, "Zookeeper")

Certainly, zoos when first conceived were little more than prisons. However, zookeeping has been undergoing a revolution for the past several decades in which older-style cages have been converted to naturalistic habitats with less visible boundaries, and space and care have been extended to allow the animals to express their natural behaviors. Allowing those behaviors has a limit, however, as zoos are required to strictly follow all animal care guidelines. So, for example, lions aren't allowed to hunt and eat live prey, due to the restrictions on care to the prey animals. (I also shudder to think of the reaction of animal rights activists to the thought of any carnivore displaying predatory behavior in view of the public—"*Think of the children!!!*")

The stated purpose of zoos has shifted from display for entertainment purposes to display for education and conservation (Patrick et al.). However, much of the public maintains the perception of zoos as animal jails. Zoos and aquariums try to counteract this belief; many zoos even have research departments to explore better management of wild populations and address conservation concerns. Supporting many of these efforts are conservation biologists and educators alike (Borrell; Moss et al.) but, so far, the momentum has been with the anti-zoo activists. There is widespread skepticism about the efforts of the zoos, with many critics dismissing those efforts outright (Fravel). This skepticism is again reflected in Zookeeper Joanna's statements:

> *Joanna:* "There is so much good a zoo does for animals, besides lock them up and examine them, which is of course just part of maintaining a natural environment for these creatures. Without the conservation efforts of the zoo, these animals would just be locked up and examined by predators."

As an added nod to our difficult relationship with animals, at the end of episode 95, Joanna shapeshifts into a large feline carnivore and eats all of her charges (well, except for the tarantulas, who have wandered off to the Human Resources department at the station and applied for jobs). Cecil notes that this seems to be a hazard of keeping animals in the zoo (as opposed to the wild), but Joanna points out that it's just her lunch.

Welcome to Night Vale is a program that celebrates and supports the anti-establishment, the weird, and the just plain offbeat. Where animals are concerned, however, it may not always be quite weird enough. While in some cases *Night Vale* bypasses our cultural attitudes toward animals (e.g., by simply presenting sentient animals with language and conscious motivations), in other cases, the underlying animal themes fit directly into well-established cultural norms and beliefs. It is unfortunate as well that often writers of science fiction and fantasy do not seem to pull from the science that explores animal thought processes and abilities as much as they could. A more varied and layered animal characterization could be an intriguing addition to the town. It is a bit disappointing, too, that Carlos, who studies so many unusual phenomena in town, has yet to really try to study any of the animals, even when Khoshekh moves into his home. It's possible this stems from yet another unconscious bias: that the study of animals and animal behavior is not "real science." Carlos, of course, represents the stereotype of a scientist: lab coat-wearing, beaker filling, detail-obsessed folks that are not very good at dealing with other living beings. Me, I'll keep to my jeans-wearing, dirty, messy, slobbery, fishy scientist ways.

NOTE

1. These examples clearly do sound like science fiction, and even clarifying the context doesn't necessarily make them easier to believe. In the case of the dolphins, the lab in which I was working was on the beach in Honolulu. People would regularly climb the walls to look at the dolphins and get yelled at to get down. The dolphins had noticed people on the wall and were vocalizing aggressively at the "intruders" and also toward us. The bonobo was a keyboard symbol-competent individual who sat and showed no evidence of distress while pointing to the symbol for "monster" and then into the woods. When I asked if there was a monster in the woods, she pointed to "bite" and gestured to the back of my neck, where I had shown her a large insect bite from earlier in the day. She then gave a small alarm call and

pointed at the woods again. The joysticks and mirrors are well documented in the literature, for example, Washburn and Rumbaugh; Rumbaugh, Richardson et al.; Reiss and Marino.

WORKS CITED

Alba, Beatrice, and Nick Haslam. "Dog People and Cat People Differ on Dominance-Related Traits." *Anthrozoös* 28, no. 1, Taylor & Francis (March 2015): 37–44. https://doi.org/10.2752/089279315X14129350721858.

Alberthsen, Corinne, et al. "Numbers and Characteristics of Cats Admitted to Royal Society for the Prevention of Cruelty to Animals (RSPCA) Shelters in Australia and Reasons for Surrender." *Animals* 6, no. 3 (2016): 1–22.

"Aquariums and Marine Parks." *People for the Ethical Treatment of Animals.* Accessed January 1, 2017. http://www.peta.org/issues/animals-in-entertainment/zoos-pseudo-sanctuaries/aquariums-marine-parks/.

Borrell, James. "Eight Reasons Why Zoos Are Good for Conservation." *Biologist* 63, no. 5 (2016): 9.

"Dog Shaming." *Dog Shaming*, 2017. http://www.dogshaming.com/.

Fravel, Laura. "Critics Question Zoos' Commitment to Conservation." *National Geographic News*, 2003. http://news.nationalgeographic.com/news/2003/11/1113_031113_zoorole.html.

Friends of the Vancouver Aquarium. Commissioner Mackinnon: "Send the Rescues Somewhere Else". http://vanaquafriends.org/2017/03/commissioner-mackinnon-send-rescues-somewhere-else/.

Gardner, R. Allen, et al. *Teaching Sign Language to Chimpanzees.* State University of New York Press, 1989.

Gordon, Joan. "Learning to Live with the Animals in SF." *Science Fiction Studies* no. 17 (2010a): 321–327.

———. "Talking (For, with) Dogs: Science Fiction Breaks a Species Barrier." *Science-Fiction Studies* 37, no. 3 (2010b): 456–465.

Gosling, Samuel D., et al. "Personalities of Self-Identified 'Dog People' and 'Cat People'." *Anthrozoös* 23, no. 3, Berg Publishers (September 2010): 213–222. https://doi.org/10.2752/175303710X12750451258850.

Harrison, F.B. "Gender and Sex." *The Journal of Education* 13, no. 4 (1891): 202–205.

Herman, Louis M., Adam A. Pack, et al. "Representational and Conceptual Skills of Dolphins." In *Language and Communication: Comparative Perspectives*, ed. Herbert L Roitblat et al., 403–442. Lawrence Erlbaum Associates, Inc., 1993.

Herman, Louis M., Stan A. Kuczaj, et al. "Responses to Anomalous Gestural Sequences by a Language-Trained Dolphin: Evidence for Processing of Semantic Relations and Syntactic Information." *Journal of Experimental Psychology: General* 122, no. 2 (1993): 184–194.

Herzog, H. *Some We Love, Some We Hate, Some We Eat: Why It's So Hard to Think Straight About Animals*. HarperCollins, 2011. https://books.google.com/books?id=5yjzWUckNIMC.

Kellogg, W.N., and L.A. Kellogg. *The Ape and the Child*. McGraw-Hill, 1933.

King, Barbara J. *Personalities on the Plate: The Lives and Minds of Animals We Eat*. University of Chicago Press, 2017.

Johnson, Kij. "The Evolution of Trickster Stories Among the Dogs of North Park After the Charge". In *At the Mouth of the River of the Bees: Stories*, 1st ed., ed. Kij Johnson. Small Beer Press, 2012.

Lewis, C.S. *The Magician's Nephew*. Collier, 1970.

Lyn, H. "Apes and the Evolution of Language: Taking Stock of 40 Years of Research." In *The Oxford Handbook of Comparative Evolutionary Psychology*, ed. J. Vonk and T. Shackelford. Oxford University Press, 2012.

———. "Mental Representation of Symbols as Revealed by Vocabulary Errors in Two Bonobos (Pan Paniscus)." *Animal Cognition* 10, no. 4 (2007): 461–475.

Lyn, H., Patricia Marks Greenfield, et al. "The Development of Representational Play in Chimpanzees and Bonobos: Evolutionary Implications, Pretense, and the Role of Interspecies Communication." *Cognitive Development* 21, no. 3 (2006): 199–213.

Lyn, H., Jamie L. Russell, et al. "The Impact of Environment on the Comprehension of Declarative Communication in Apes." *Psychological Science* 21, no. 3 (April 29, 2010): 360–365. https://doi.org/10.1177/0956797610362218.

Lyn, H., and Sue Savage-Rumbaugh. "The Use of Emotion Symbols in Language-Using Apes." In *Emotions of Animals and Humans: Comparative Perspectives*, ed. Shigeru Watanabe and Stan Kuczaj, 113–128, Springer, 2013.

"Marine Mammals in Captivity." *The Humane Society of the United States*. Accessed January 1, 2017. http://www.humanesociety.org/issues/captive_marine/facts/marine_captivity.html?credit=web.

Martin, Rod A. *The Psychology of Humor: An Integrative Approach*. Academic Press, 2010.

McKechnie, Claire Charlotte, and John Miller. "Victorian Animals." *Journal of Victorian Culture* 17, no. 4 (2012): 436–441. https://doi.org/10.1080/13555502.2012.735448.

Mitchell, Robert W., and Alan L. Ellis. "Cat Person, Dog Person, Gay, or Heterosexual: The Effect of Labels on a Man's Perceived Masculinity, Femininity, and Likability." *Society & Animals: Journal of Human-Animal Studies* 21, no. 1 (2013): 1–16. https://doi.org/10.1163/15685306-12341266.

Moss, Andrew, et al. "Evaluating the Contribution of Zoos and Aquariums to Aichi Biodiversity Target 1." *Conservation Biology* 29, no. 2 (2015): 537–544.

Nelson, Julie. *Economics as Social Theory: Feminism, Objectivity and Economics*. Routledge, 1995.

NOAA (National Oceanic and Atmospheric Administration) Fisheries. *Special Report: Southern Resident Killer Whales, 10 Years of Research and Conservation*, 2014. https://www.nwfsc.noaa.gov/news/features/killer_whale_report/.

Pate, James L., and Duane M. Rumbaugh. "The Language-like Behavior of Lana Chimpanzee: Is It Merely Discrimination and Paired-Associate Learning?" *Animal Learning and Behavior* 11, no. 1 (1983): 134–138.

Patrick, Patricia G., et al. "Conservation and Education: Prominent Themes in Zoo Mission Statements." *The Journal of Environmental Education* 38, no. 3 (2007): 53–60. https://doi.org/10.3200/JOEE.38.3.53-60.

Patterson, Francine G., and Eugene Linden. *The Education of Koko*. Holt, Rinehart and Winston, 1981.

Pepperberg, Irene M. *The Alex Studies: Cognitive and Communicative Abilities of Grey Parrots*. Harvard University Press, 1999.

Reiss, Diana L., and Lori Marino. "Mirror Self-Recognition in the Bottlenose Dolphin: A Case of Cognitive Convergence." *Proceedings of the National Academy of Sciences of the United States of America* 98, no. 10 (2001): 5937–5942.

Robeck, Todd, et al. "Scientific Correspondence: Killer Whale (Orcinus Orca) Survivorship in Captivity: A Critique of Jett and Ventre (2015) Scientific Correspondence: Killer Whale (Orcinus Orca) Survivorship in Captivity: A Critique of Jett and Ventre (2015)." *Marine Mammal Science* 32, no. 2 (2016): 786–792.

Rumbaugh, Duane M., et al. "Rhesus Monkeys (Macaca Mulatta), Video Tasks, and Implications for Stimulus-Response Spatial Contiguity." *Journal of Comparative Psychology* 103, no. 1 (1989): 32–38.

Savage-Rumbaugh, E. Sue, and Roger Lewin. *Kanzi: The Ape at the Brink of the Human Mind*. John Wiley and Sons, Inc., 1994.

Serpell, J. *The Domestic Dog: Its Evolution, Behavior and Interaction with People*. Cambridge University Press, 1995.

Unicorns-at-arbys. "43 – Visitor – Comment." *Podbay*. http://podbay.fm/show/536258179/e/1394856000?autostart=1.

Vint, Sherryl. "'The Animals in That Country': Science Fiction and Animal Studies." *Science Fiction Studies* 35, no. 2 (2008): 177–188.

Washburn, David A., and Duane M. Rumbaugh. "Testing Primates with Joystick-Based Automated Apparatus." *Behavior Research Methods, Instruments and Computers* 24, no. 2 (1992): 157–164.

CHAPTER 5

"It Would Make More Sense for It to Be There Than Not": Constructing Night Vale as a "Place"

Andy McCumber

Abstract Within the interdisciplinary literature on the construction of place, many scholars have paid special attention to the role of narrative and storytelling. However, this perspective has not been duly applied to fictional places in contemporary media as a tool for cultural analysis. In this chapter, I draw on work from cultural geographers, sociologists, anthropologists, and literary critics to bring an analysis of place to *Welcome to Night Vale*. I analyze how multiple, sometimes contradictory, imaginations of Night Vale, which combine to form an overarching sense of the town as a place, are constructed through narrative. I argue that the construction of Night Vale as a place happens through narrative, both in the sense of the format of the episodes themselves and in the sense of a shared participation in the story by *Night Vale*'s fans.

Keywords Narrative • Place • Social space • Virtuality

A. McCumber (✉)
University of California, Santa Barbara, CA, USA
e-mail: ahmccumber@ucsb.edu

© The Author(s) 2018
J. A. Weinstock (ed.), *Critical Approaches to* Welcome to Night Vale,
https://doi.org/10.1007/978-3-319-93091-6_5

In the Desert Creek housing development in the town of Night Vale there is a house that does not exist. "It seems like it exists. Like it's just right there when you look at it," explains Cecil Palmer, the narrator in the popular fiction podcast *Welcome to Night Vale*, adding "it's between two other identical houses, so it would make more sense for it to be there than not" (Fink and Cranor, *Mostly Void* 252). Nonetheless, the house does not exist, confounding a team of scientific researchers who are sent to investigate it.

The nonexistent house is a recurring bit in *Welcome to Night Vale*, one that exemplifies the show's absurdist and existential humor. Additionally though, Night Vale residents' relationship to the house might be thought of as a negative image of the relationship that listeners of the show have with the fictional town itself. The house is "right there when you look at it" but, according to Night Vale's bizarre cosmic rules, it does not exist. On the other hand, listeners never see Night Vale. They suspend disbelief as the world of the town is conjured primarily in the words they get from a single authority, Cecil. In this respect, it would, contrary to the house, "make more sense" for Night Vale to *not* be there than to be there. Yet this fictional town has achieved a concreteness with its audience that emplaces it in much the same way that an actual physical geographic spot might be emplaced.

Place is the subject of a rich interdisciplinary literature that theorizes our cognitive experience of the world and the processes through which we give it social meaning. Place is generally the intersection of the physical and the social; it is co-constituted by the two. This chapter uses Night Vale to ask how we might use the framework developed by scholars to describe meaning-making in the physical-geographical, concrete world and apply it to fictional places that exist in the ether of our collective imaginations. One of its goals is to argue for the inclusion of certain kinds of fictional towns, cities, and worlds into our understanding of place. Through the example of Night Vale, I will discuss how fiction, particularly as an ongoing event that allows for some degree of participation by consumers, applies a place-making process to these locales that is essentially the same as that which makes place out of physical spots.

The other goal of the chapter is more specific to Night Vale. I will discuss how Night Vale owes its potency as a place to factors related to the specific social context in which it exists. The format of the show, its sense of humor, and its subject matter all conspire to make *Welcome to Night Vale* a uniquely social experience for listeners. This social element of the podcast is key to the emplacement of Night Vale. Furthermore, I will argue that the place created in Night Vale out of this process achieves its clarity by embodying a set of contradictions that correspond with the desires and anxieties of the audience it reaches.

The chapter will proceed in three parts. First, I will review the literature on place to answer the fundamental question of whether Night Vale, a fictional town, qualifies as a place under this framework. Much of the work on this topic has emphasized the social qualities of place over the innately physical, and I proceed from there to argue that Night Vale is constructed in much the same way "real" places are. This extension of the concept of place has the potential to meaningfully expand our understanding of peoples' cultural relationship to physical and social space. In the next section I will discuss the particular characteristics of the show that make the listening experience a social one, using a few foundational works in the discipline of sociology and the study of social interaction to make this point. I argue that, given the social nature of place-construction, the unique role played by listeners of the podcast gives the fictional town its potency as a place. For this reason I believe *Night Vale* exemplifies both a new and unique social form of narrative and, by extension, a new mode of place-based community making capable of playing out in the ether of our collective imaginations. Finally, the last section will turn to the relationship between Night Vale and its audience on a more macro-scale and examine how Night Vale speaks to its listeners by capturing the cultural-political condition of the particular milieu it reaches, a requisite accomplishment for place-creation in fiction.

DRAWING THE BOUNDARIES OF "PLACE"

The literature on the construction of place emerged out of several different scholarly conversations spanning various disciplines and intellectual traditions. Early contributors came from cultural geography, sociology, anthropology, and more, and often articulated the concept of place using different vocabularies. As such, place is a contested concept with multiple possible interpretations, and different lines drawn around what exactly constitutes place. Many scholars have focused their attention specifically on the interactions between people and their physical environments, viewing place as created out of this give and take. We impose social, personal, and emotional meaning on parts of the world to order our experiences of it. For these scholars, place may be social but it is also undeniably material and physical, which would seem to disqualify fictional places like Night Vale. For Michel de Certeau, for instance, even in the planned and managed environments of cities, place only takes shape through the practice of navigating the streets as a pedestrian, using, modifying, and transcending the space of the urban grid (91–110). Similarly, philosopher Edward Casey theorizes place as created in the bodily experience of navigating abstract "space."

Similarly, environmental sociologists have contributed to the discussion around place-construction in ways that affirm the importance of the bio-physical "stuff" out of which place is made (see, e.g., Catton and Dunlap; Dunlap and Catton; Murphy and Dunlap). William Freudenburg, Scott Frickel, and Robert Gramling write of the many potential senses of place that might be socially constructed and applied to a mountain but point out how each of them is undeniably tied to the physical properties of the mountain itself. These scholars deploy the concept of place to bring the physical environment into sociological analysis and push back against the orthodoxy of a discipline that sits at the other extreme, where phenomena are to be explained only by the social. Another sociologist, Thomas Gieryn, in a review article that argues for greater engagement with place in sociology, states explicitly that place is "[not] to be found in cyberspace" (465), essentially precluding fictional towns like Night Vale from being emplaced.

But other definitions of the concept do not emphasize the material as strongly. Place may be seen as co-constituted dialectically by the physical-geographical and the social, but scholars often articulate the power of the social to create place in a way that supersedes the backdrop provided by the physical. In *Space and Place*, a foundational work in this literature, cultural geographer Yi-Fu Tuan writes that a sense of familiarity, and a related investment of "value," is the defining factor that transforms "space" into place (Tuan 6). Similarly, Marc Augé writes that "place is completed through the word, through the allusive exchange of a few passwords," where "aphorisms, vocabulary, and modes of thought form a cosmology" (Augé 77). For these authors, place takes shape where there is a shared understanding, especially one communicated socially, which is what Keith Basso observed in Western Apache peoples' construction of place names in his book *Wisdom Sits in Places*. It is not a stretch to imagine that same familiarity taking root for real people in a fictional place like Night Vale.

In fact, some take this emphasis on language and mutually understood meaning further by suggesting that narrative, as in folklore, is key to creating place. Kent Ryden writes that "place is in fact as much a verbal as a physical or geographical phenomenon," and, quoting Barbara Johnstone, that "our sense of place ... is rooted in narration. A person is at home in a place when the place evokes stories and, conversely, stories can serve to create places" (42). His analysis of place still focuses on our experiences of the material world, but he writes of an "invisible landscape" of social meaning superimposed on the physical one. And even Ryden can imagine how the "invisible landscape" might exist without directly corresponding with the lived, material landscape. He discusses a map included in William Faulkner's *Absalom, Absalom!* of the fictional Yoknapatawpha County, where most of his books take place. Ryden says of this map, which is annotated to show the locations of events from several of Faulkner's novels: "Faulkner has created ... a fictional imitation of any town or county where people have accumulated histories; he has done in fictional form what many people could do orally for their own towns after having spent many years living and listening there" (47). Yoknapatawpha County reads as if it is a real, physical locale because of the detail Faulkner has given it, but also because of its relatability. It roughly resembles the actual Lafayette County, Faulkner's home, so, while fictional, it is closely linked to the real world. In this way it captures the history and lived experience of people close to the stories Faulkner tells, or to use Raymond Williams' famous definition of culture, the structure of feeling (128–135) of a region and a population.

Recent work in cultural geography has further theorized the tangibility of place that is divorced from the physical-geographical world. The term "fictive place," coined by John Overton and Warwick Murray, is the topic of work investigating the production of places through ideas and associations that may take hold despite lacking substantive connection to the physical location in question (see Overton and Murray; Murray and Overton; Masuda and Bookman), in the same way the collective memory of a person, as discussed by sociologist Barry Schwartz, can be much more related to a sociocultural imagination than to their lived reality. In a way, these approaches further the goal of Henri Lefebvre (11–12) of a "unitary theory" of space capable of bridging physical, mental, and social conceptions of space. Place is created socially, and through a process that calls into question any clear distinction between real and imagined. Night Vale can be understood through the lens of this work, which indicates how fictional places might be conjured in the same way we emplace "real" ones or vice versa.

Welcome to Night Vale similarly creates a vivid place removed from the material world, whose potency is nonetheless derived from social processes unfolding through real lived experience. Rather than corresponding directly with a real desert town, however, Night Vale is emplaced through a narrative that captures the sensibilities of a widely dispersed listenership. This gives it its own relatability. The following sections will discuss in more detail specifically how Night Vale is emplaced and what gives it its potency in its specific cultural-historical context.

How Is Night Vale Emplaced?

Granting that the imagined worlds of fiction can become "places" does not mean assuming that every fictional town becomes so emplaced. Place is a social phenomenon, and *Welcome to Night Vale* is unique in its ability to tap into the social process of place-creation. What shapes Night Vale in the minds of listeners are, oddly, not its elements that are common to the average southwestern desert town, but those elements that are strange to the point of being difficult to imagine. These surreal elements of Night Vale read as a kind of regional folklore almost exclusively told from the point of view of Cecil's news dispatches from his community radio show. The show has expanded to include different voice actors and narrating perspectives, but Cecil is its bedrock. Night Vale is emplaced through the straightforward descriptions of the town that he gives, but also through more subtle nuanced elements of his show that convey emotion, establish sometimes bizarre social norms, and build a set of cultural dispositions with substantial depth. In this respect, Night Vale unfolds in the same way the world of an improv comedy sketch develops between actors on stage trained never to reject or contradict any input. The surreal quality of the town violates basic understandings of the world, ranging from scientific facts to deeply rooted cultural norms, so when Cecil introduces them, they require a unique engagement on behalf of listeners, who must buy in, no matter how strange things get.

One of the most illustrative examples of the bizarre elements that make Night Vale what it is happens in the show's second episode, titled "Glow Cloud." The title storyline from this episode revolves around a glowing cloud that envelops Night Vale, inexplicably dropping animals of various kinds onto the town below. Cecil reports matter-of-factly about the cloud, save for a brief moment when he becomes entranced and begins compulsively worshiping it. The Glow Cloud returns in a later episode, titled

"The Lights in Radon Canyon," when it takes up residence in Night Vale, ultimately becoming the president of the local school board.

This storyline is quintessential Night Vale in that many absurd aspects are introduced with no explanation. The show never probes deeper into why or how a glowing cloud would materialize and drop animal carcasses over a desert town. Nor does it give any information to help listeners understand its shift to presenting the cloud as an anthropomorphized citizen capable of serving on the school board. One of *Night Vale*'s creators, Jeffrey Cranor, writes in the introduction to the script for "Glow Cloud" in the collection *Mostly Void, Partially Stars* that this storyline helped both writers and listeners "wrap [their] heads around what Night Vale is" (Fink and Cranor 10) by establishing this set of rules, where the most bizarre events have to be accepted: "Oh, there's a giant glowing cloud that controls our minds and drops dead animals, and we don't know where it came from, and where it's going, and we're scared of its capabilities but not horrified by its very existence? Got it. Totally. Let's do this" (Fink and Cranor, *Mostly Void, Partially Stars* 11). This disposition is a prerequisite for being a listener of the show. Without it, *Night Vale* is just a frustrating, confusing stream of nonsense that offers no satisfactory explanation.

The listener's experience of Night Vale in these absurd instances is a social one. In *Building Imaginary Worlds*, Mark J.P. Wolf contends that collaboratively constructed worlds come to exist independently of the narratives that take place in them (17). While Night Vale is constructed through narrative, it is this collaborative element whereby listeners participate by accepting the town's eccentricities at face value that shapes it in listeners' imaginations. As Tuan, Augé, and others emphasize, place is borne out of social processes that create shared understandings and meaning. With that in mind, we can interpret Night Vale's absurdities in terms of what Emile Durkheim, the father of modern sociology, termed "social facts." Durkheim defined this term this way: "A social fact is any way of acting, whether fixed or not, capable of exerting over the individual an external constraint" (27). From the listener's perspective, these bizarre norms are violations of the social facts that exist in their own world.

In fact, they call to mind the work of another scholar of social interaction, Harold Garfinkel. Garfinkel called his way of interrogating the fundamentals of social interactions ethnomethodology, and his research often involved deliberately breaking basic social norms in a Night Valean manner. These violations of social expectations were called "breaching experiments." In a famous example, Garfinkel describes an experiment where the researcher challenges a subject to a game of tic-tac-toe and invites them to make the first move. When they do so, he erases their move and changes it to a different square before responding with his. The subjects tended to respond to this by assuming the researcher's actions had little to do with the game of tic-tac-toe and instead indicated they had some ulterior motive (a sexual advance, an insult to their intelligence, etc.) (Garfinkel 71–72). Rarely did they interpret the breach simply as an indication that the game they were playing was not the tic-tac-toe they were familiar with; even when the rules plainly did not apply, they remain stable in our minds and we interpret apparent transgressions in terms of them.

But while parts of the podcast resemble these breaching experiments, such as when Cecil violates the listener's expectation of what "a word from our sponsors" refers to by launching into an extended soliloquy that reads as a non sequitur, a key part of being a Night Vale listener is playing along, accepting the reality Cecil presents. This goes beyond the normal call to suspend one's disbelief that is implicit in any work of fiction, because the absurdities often do not even make sense within the world of the show, except for the agreed-upon rule that anything is fair game. This is the overarching social fact that governs the listening experience of *Welcome to Night Vale*, and it is this social component of the show that makes Night Vale so vividly emplaced. While entirely new social facts emerge in the world of the show, the listener plays an important role of accepting them as they come. They participate in the creation of the world by agreeing to its rules and this serves to emplace Night Vale for them.

Absurd and Close to Home: Night Vale and the "Real World"

In this way, Night Vale is constructed in terms of a central contradiction between its own rules and those of its listeners' world. The tension between the two is explicitly written into the show, in the form of Night Vale's tenuous relationship to the "real world." One of the podcast's biggest "breaches" of common sense expectations occurs in the contradictory reminders Cecil gives us, on the one hand, of Night Vale's relationship to the real world (we are told it is in the American southwest somewhere, and references are made to real historical events), and on the other hand its paranormal disconnectedness from the world beyond. Arrivals into Night Vale's Randy Newman Memorial Airport, for instance, are unscheduled surprises to "both pilots and air traffic control" and take "routes that appear to violate the simple laws of physics and geography" (Fink and Cranor, *Mostly Void* 152–54). People wander into Night Vale by accident and lose track of time as it relates to the lives they left behind (Fink and Cranor, *Mostly Void* 112–20).

This is the overarching contradiction that defines Night Vale, but the town is also riddled with internal contradictions, which unexpectedly serve to form tangible connections between it and the sociocultural reality of its real-world listeners and creators. Night Vale is part close-knit small town, yet part impersonal authoritarian regime, part postmodern corporate dystopia, yet part beacon of progressivism and social acceptance. What might read as continuity errors to some are probably better interpreted as a broad, nuanced commentary on a variety of social conditions. Just as Night Vale is a dialectical co-constitution of material reality and the absurd possibilities of the imagined, it is also the embodiment of a dialectic between the anxieties and desires of the social milieu that conspires to create it in the first place.

Cecil introduces us to Night Vale's cast of characters in a way that gives an impression of the town as a small, familiar community. He refers to Larry Leroy out on the edge of town, John Peters ("you know, the farmer?"), and Old Woman Josie as if listeners are already well aware of these personas by virtue of supposedly living in Night Vale. Cecil himself plays the role of a "public character," an idea introduced by Jane Jacobs and further theorized by urban ethnographer Mitch Duneier that describes a person who holds a community together by making investments in many of its members' lives and generally looking out for their best interests. On the other hand, Cecil makes casual references to "the Arby's" and "the Ralph's," among other corporate chains, which make Night Vale seem more sterile and impersonal. The tension between these two sides of Night Vale reflects the ever-increasing ability to connect with others in the modern technological world, and the increasing mediation of those connections and steady encroachment into various facets of our lives by corporate entities. This interplay in Night Vale calls to mind the work of theorists who suggest corporate homogeneity steadily converts place into "nonplace" (Augé) or "placelessness" (Relph; Glassberg). In the podcast, this worry comes to a head in a plotline where Night Vale is taken over by a company called "StrexCorp."

The overthrow of this corporate villain reads as an unambiguous victory for Night Vale, yet before and after that Night Vale is nonetheless also consistently characterized by a matter-of-fact acceptance of state violence and authoritarian rule. The town seems to live in a state of casual and perpetual fear of their town's authority figures who are numerous and powerful, if at times comically inept. Cecil frequently refers to a "vague yet menacing government agency," which epitomizes real-world fears that the most powerful levels of government both lack transparency and lack the best interests of ordinary citizens in their motives. Other Orwellian elements of Night Vale include ubiquitous and intrusive surveillance programs and the "sheriff's secret police."

These all conspire to paint an image of Night Vale as a repressed police state, which forms one half of a contradiction that provides undertones to the show that position it politically. This is accomplished despite the fact that it rarely takes an overt political stance with respect to real-world issues. Creator Joseph Fink even teased the audience with an introduction to the September 30, 2016, episode "Zookeeper" (episode 95) that began "Big election season, right now, huh? Boy am I not going to talk about any of that." But while neither the creators nor Cecil may come out and "talk about" those issues directly, the podcast frequently makes reference to potent items of cultural-political discourse. A recent episode, for example, centered on the opening of a new landfill in Night Vale where residents can dispose of esoteric, immaterial items like thoughts and feelings. While discussing the guidelines for disposal at this new facility, Cecil references the widespread disdain that many expressed for the year of 2016, particularly after the election of Donald Trump. He advises that, while it is possible to throw out an entire year at the landfill, he cautions that "a year that seems uniquely terrible, could, in fact, be merely the gateway to an era of terror—the launching point and not the peak" (episode 101, "Guidelines for Disposal").

Night Vale also embodies a general sentiment around acceptance, characterized, for example, by Cecil's assertion that that five-headed dragon ought to have the right to run for public office (Fink and Cranor, *Mostly Void* 107–108). At times, the show conveys this sentiment in ways that reference real-world social justice issues. A prime example is the Apache Tracker, a character whose caricaturistic faux-Native American garb Cecil is offended by, and who remains a "racist embarrassment" to the town even after becoming a town hero (Fink and Cranor, *Great Glowing Coils* 16). This statement about cultural appropriation is fairly overt, but there are other subtler statements made, such as the show's acknowledgment of gender fluidity in its introduction of Sam, the sheriff who is referred to only using gender-neutral pronouns.

The tension between "Sheriff Sam" and "the sheriff's secret police," so to speak, makes Night Vale a vivid place because it is derived from the social reality of the show's audience. Even without access to more detailed data on the show's listenership, it is safe to say that *Welcome to Night Vale* appeals to a demographic whose sensibilities lie outside of the mainstream. The show's online store offers merchandise marketed toward self-identified oddballs, such as shorts labeled "creepy" on the behind, and a shirt with the mantra "weird at last, weird at last, god almighty, weird at last." "Weird," of course is an imperfect stand-in for "queer," for example, or any other more specific, more politically charged self-identification, but those two are linked heavily in the construction of Night Vale as a place. It is no accident that a show with its bizarre, absurdist sensibilities also features an ambiguously gendered sheriff who prefers neutral pronouns—and a radio host who respectfully obliges for that matter. The "weird at last" ethos of the show and its audience is connected to a general desire for acceptance, and particularly acceptance of those people who have been marginalized in some way for their difference. These are real-world concerns that give the fictional Night Vale life. To the show's audience, the town provides a celebration of difference and a commentary on the forces that threaten it.

Pierre Bourdieu theorizes the role of contradictions in producing place in *Outline of a Theory of Practice*, writing that a set of oppositions (hot versus cold, male versus female, light versus shade, and more) gave a logic to the organization of the indigenous Kabyle houses he observed in his fieldwork and Algeria, and that "the same oppositions are established between the house as a whole and the rest of the universe" (90). It is likewise oppositions that emplace Night Vale. The town is composed of tensions between difference and imposed homogeneity, the absurd and the familiar, freedom and repression, even place and placelessness. These contradictions order the social experience of being a Night Vale listener, making the town vivid in their imaginations, even in its surreal un-imaginability.

Conclusion

Place promises to remain a contested concept, characterized by ongoing debates over what lies within and outside of its framework. The particular debate over whether place is necessarily rooted in the material "real" world is likely to become even more contentious though, as we continue to imagine places and connect socially through diverse and changing mediums. Theorists of the postmodern turn, who have variously told us that the material conditions of our world are becoming increasingly textual (Barber) and that our mode of production is "predominantly concerned with the production of signs, images, and sign systems" (Harvey, paraphrasing Jean Baudrillard), have indicated a world where place becomes increasingly immaterial. The more mediated our experience of the world becomes as our social worlds become ever more vastly interconnected, the further we push along the project of creating places in the ether, rather than the dirt and stone.

In *Night Vale*, we find the promise of this project, which figures to become increasingly relevant in our time. The combining of the practice of creating more connected social worlds and the older practice of taking refuge in fiction will facilitate the creation of more imagined places made potent by sociocultural meaning invested in them like this paranormal desert town. Place is a constantly evolving concept, and this podcast indicates the potential of the imagination to push its boundaries even further, in ways that will demand the attention of scholars interested in place-creation. Night Vale synthesizes the essence of a shared social condition into a bizarre and imagined world. Its undeniable weirdness and its internal contradictions have potency because of the contradictory existence so many people live out in the "real world." It exemplifies pitfalls of that "real world" and utopian daydreams of what it might become without oversimplifying either. Night Vale is a place, and for all these reasons its audience is grateful for that fact.

WORKS CITED

Augé, Marc. *Non-Places: Introduction to an Anthropology of Supermodernity*. Verso, 1995.

Barber, Benjamin. *Jihad vs. McWorld: Terrorism's Challenge to Democracy*. Random House, 2010.

Basso, Keith H. *Wisdom Sits in Places: Landscape and Language Among the Western Apache*. University of New Mexico Press, 1996.

Bourdieu, Pierre. *Outline of a Theory of Practice*. Cambridge University Press, 1977.

Casey, Edward S. *Getting Back Into Place: Toward a Renewed Understanding of the Place-World*. Indiana University Press, 1993.

Catton, William R., and Riley Dunlap. "A New Ecological Paradigm for Post-Exuberant Sociology." *The American Behavioral Scientist* 24, no. 1 (1980): 15–47.

de Certeau, Michel. *The Practice of Everyday Life*. University of California Press, 1984.

Duneier, Mitchell, and Ovie Carter. *Sidewalk*. Farrar, Straus and Giroux, 2001.

Dunlap, Riley E., and William R. Catton. "What Environmental Sociologists Have in Common (Whether Concerned with 'Built' or 'Natural' Environments)." *Sociological Inquiry* 53, no. 2–3 (April 1983): 113–135.

Durkheim, Emile. *The Rules of Sociological Method: And Selected Texts on Sociology and Its Method*. Simon and Schuster, 2014.

Fink, Joseph, and Jeffrey Cranor. *The Great Glowing Coils of the Universe: Welcome to Night Vale Episodes, Volume 2*. Harper Perennial, 2016a.

———. *Mostly Void, Partially Stars: Welcome to Night Vale Episodes, Volume 1*. Harper Perennial, 2016b.

Garfinkel, Harold. *Studies in Ethnomethodology*. Prentice Hall, 1967.

Gieryn, Thomas F. "A Space for Place in Sociology." *Annual Review of Sociology* 26 (2000): 463–496.

Glassberg, David. *Sense of History: The Place of the Past in American Life*. University of Massachusetts Press, 2001.

Harvey, David. *The Condition of Postmodernity: An Enquiry into the Origins of Cultural Change*. Wiley, 1992.

Jacobs, Jane. *The Death and Life of Great American Cities*. Vintage Books, 1961.

Lefebvre, Henri. *The Production of Space*. Blackwell, 1991.

Masuda, Jeffrey R., and Sonia Bookman. "Neighbourhood Branding and the Right to the City." *Progress in Human Geography* 42, no. 2 (forthcoming): 165–182.

Murphy, Raymond, and Riley E. Dunlap. "Beyond the Society/Nature Divide: Building on the Sociology of William Freudenburg." *Journal of Environmental Studies and Sciences* 2, no. 1 (2012): 7–17.

Murray, Warwick E., and John Overton. "Fictive Clusters: Crafty Strategies in the New Zealand Beer Industry." *Norsk Geografisk Tidsskrift – Norwegian Journal of Geography* 70, no. 3 (2016): 176–189.

Overton, John, and Warwick E. Murray. "Fictive Place." *Progress in Human Geography* 40, no. 6 (forthcoming): 794.

Relph, Edward C. *Place and Placelessness*. Pion Limited, 1976.

Ryden, Kent C. *Mapping the Invisible Landscape: Folklore, Writing, and the Sense of Place*. University of Iowa Press, 1993.

Schwartz, Barry. *Lincoln and the Forge of National Memory*. University of Chicago Press, 2000.

Tuan, Yi-Fu. *Space and Place: The Perspective of Experience*. University of Minnesota Press, 1978.

Williams, Raymond. *Marxism and Literature*. Oxford University Press, 1977.

Wolf, Mark J.P. *Building Imaginary Worlds: The Theory and History of Subcreation*. Routledge, 2014.

CHAPTER 6

"More Reassuring Noise in This Quiet World": Narrative Intimacy and the Acousmatic Voice of *Night Vale*

Grace Gist

Abstract Being an acousmatic presence—a disembodied voice—Cecil lends himself to an unusual relationship with the listener as often the only voice illustrating the goings-on of the odd desert town of Night Vale. And as this narrator, several things play into his distance from the listener: in-world he is a reporter, but is also an opinionated fallible person; as a narrative device there is audio's natural and unusual intimacy; and in between those two spheres there is the fact that very little distinction is made between the character Cecil Palmer and his actor Cecil Baldwin. All of these forces shift his narrative distance, and it is through this lens that I illustrate how that distance affects the story and the listener, particularly in the events of *Welcome to Night Vale*'s second year's Strex arc.

Keywords Distance • Proximity • Sound • Voice

G. Gist (⊠)
Simmons College, Boston, MA, USA

© The Author(s) 2018
J. A. Weinstock (ed.), *Critical Approaches to* Welcome to Night Vale,
https://doi.org/10.1007/978-3-319-93091-6_6

> *Listeners, here's something weird. (Fink and Cranor,* Great Glowing
> Coils 55)

Part of what makes *Welcome to Night Vale* unusual is the shifting relationship that exists between Cecil, the disembodied voice of Night Vale community radio, and the news that he reports. In keeping with conventional news reporting, Cecil often plays the usual role of objective reporter. Then at times he adopts the role of commentator, offering his subjective appraisal of events. This is less common in contemporary news reporting, but certainly not unheard of. What the listener quickly comes to realize, however, is that Cecil is not only the narrator of events in Night Vale, but also their primary subject. That is, what initially presents itself as a third-person narrative ends up as a kind of first-person account as Cecil shifts from objective news reporter to commentator to a character central to the story he is reporting. This chapter illustrates how narrative intimacy or "proximity" between Cecil and the listener is established; in what ways his narrative distance from events change, and how such changes affect both his narration and the listener; and how these changes contribute to the longer-term narrative destabilization of the StrexCorp takeover arc. *Welcome to Night Vale* finally becomes Cecil's story in the dual sense of Cecil as both teller and subject of the tale he tells. This diminishing of narrative distance between Cecil and the events he reports is accompanied by a similar decrease in distance between Cecil and the listener as psychic identification is effected: Because Cecil's story becomes increasingly personal, intimacy is established and we become invested in the narrative. *Night Vale*'s success thus depends upon the voice of Night Vale becoming not just a voice but an intimate presence.

To begin with, as strange as *Night Vale* is, arguably very little effort on the part of the listener is needed to suspend disbelief. Much of this can be attributed to Cecil and his narrative proximity to the listener, which is established through several of his features both as a narrator and as a radio host. On the broadest level, engaging with narratives at all is itself a participatory venture, especially when the narrative is viewed as a conversation into which the reader or listener may subsequently enter. Viewed this way, the reader or listener is a side participant, someone not directly involved with the conversation itself at the present moment but who is invited and expected to gather and understand the conversation's information to prepare for potential involvement (Polichak 72–74). Using details in the narrative provided either directly or indirectly, the listener can take cues from the narrative structure and piece the story together both factually and emotionally (Oatley 45–50).

Sound itself also demands participation. Jean-Luc Nancy discusses sound in a broader, philosophical sense, and describes listening as hearing a sound, figuring out its meaning, and making sense of those two things together (7). That act, along with the near instantaneous relationship between sound and the listener, suggests that sound is participatory by nature (10). Nancy's particular examples are music, but his meditations certainly apply to verbal sound as well. Concerning radio drama in particular, Neil Verma describes trends and techniques used to position the listener and establish narrative proximity within American radio dramas of the late 1930s (35). Some dramas would situate the listener "equidistant" from all of the characters, presenting the narrative from an egalitarian third-person omniscient point of view; Verma calls this sort of positioning kaleidosonic (65, 68). At the other end of the spectrum, intimate positioning places the listener alongside one or two characters throughout a story (58), and in many cases this aural favoring of one character over others lends itself to sympathetic attachment to that character and their particular perspective (59–60). In *Night Vale*, especially during the first two years, the listener hears Cecil almost exclusively, both as narrator and character, and thus has this intimate proximity to him. And so from the outset, by virtue of *Night Vale*'s nature as narrative in sound, the listener arguably is brought even "closer" to the narrator than in a written text.

Night Vale, as listeners know, is presented using the structure of a fairly typical news broadcast conveyed by a single voice on the radio. Such voices can be described as acousmatic, or coming from someone who is invisible to the listener or otherwise disembodied (Granly). This acousmatic nature of radio and the use of a format that emphasizes a voice that often directly addresses its listeners lend themselves to a close connection between the listener and the voice. That direct connection and the listener's role in constructing something with whatever that voice provides—in Cecil's case, constructing Night Vale as a place (see McCumber in this volume), its events as something of a plot, and Cecil as a character—creates a curious relationship between the listener and the voice on the radio who becomes familiar despite being in reality a stranger. Outside of fiction, anecdotal evidence suggests this relationship can also apply to actual and more conventionally "objective" radio voices like news anchors or interviewers. In March 2014, America's National Public Radio (NPR) announced longtime broadcaster Carl Kasell's retirement (Peralta). The article cited a statement from NPR's vice president of programming, Eric Nuzum, describing Kasell in his newscaster role for *Morning Edition*: "He was the voice people woke up to. They opened their eyes, and for 30 years, he was there, reassuring them the world was still in one piece." A brief glance at the comments section following the article shows an outpouring of reminiscences from listeners who talk about how connected they felt to Kasell's acousmatic presence. In a more humorous depiction of this phenomenon, Eleanor Davis illustrates a listener's connection with the main voice of NPR's *Fresh Air* in a *New Yorker* comic, with the title itself suggesting the sort of relationship: "Who Needs Friends When You've Got Terry Gross?" Radio commentators to whom we listen to regularly become our "friends," despite the facts that we've never met and can't really talk with them.

As a community radio announcer, Cecil exists in something of a gray area between newscaster and personality. He reads the news reports for Night Vale happenings, such as reporting the opening of a new Dog Park:

> The City Council announces the opening of a new Dog Park at the corner of Earl and Somerset, near the Ralphs. They would like to remind everyone that dogs are not allowed in the Dog Park. People are not allowed in the Dog Park. ... Do not approach the Dog Park. The fence is electrified and highly dangerous. ... The Dog Park will not harm you. (Fink and Cranor, *Mostly Void* 3)

But he will also go off on more personal, poetic tangents, as well as minor personal tirades. Consider Cecil's coverage of the debate surrounding revitalization of Night Vale's Old Town Drawbridge in episode 6 ("The Drawbridge"):

> One critic, who wished to remain anonymous, said, "We don't even have a river or bay in Night Vale. There would never be a boat to necessitate a drawbridge." He continued to...
> You know what? Forget it. I can tell you right now that that was Steve Carlsberg who said that. And he is such a spoilsport, that Steve. Have you noticed how he never replaces his hubcaps? It's laziness. Pure and simple. Laziness. I just can't let him ruin our town by denying Night Vale a drawbridge when he can't even care for a tan Corolla. (Fink and Cranor, *Mostly Void* 51)

What begins as conventional news reporting here quickly—and comically—slips into subjective invective against Steve Carlsberg, a persistent object of Cecil's scorn.

Whether Cecil is objective or subjective, in listening to him the listener engages in a weird, one-sided pen-pal relationship through the course of the series. Cecil provides various bits of information—about the town, the story, and himself—and the listeners assemble that information into pictures of Night Vale, its residents, and Cecil in their mind. A direct connection is established between the listener and Cecil, magnified by radio's immediacy.

Night Vale, one should mention, isn't alone in these narrative peculiarities; other audio series explore the relationship between narrative voice, the listener, and the events of the story. Some do this through traditional narrators, such as the corporate narrator in *Our Fair City*, whose characters' stories of rebellion conflict with the narrator's exhortations to loyalty; others tell stories through audio that also exists in the story world itself, such as *The Bright Sessions* and *ars Paradoxica*, and listener consideration of why this found footage exists the way that it does can shape their experience with the narrative. However, what distinguishes *Night Vale* is that the primary narrative voice—the single voice through whom the world of Night Vale is built, while situated in close proximity to the listener—is also a character within that world, and subject to the events within it. This overlap of functions allows for intense intimacy between Cecil and the listener, with the potential for eliciting powerful affective response.

The listener's intimacy with Cecil then inflects how we respond to the news he reports. Because we know Cecil and Cecil knows Night Vale, we can trust his evaluations of events, which allows news that might in the "real world" terrify us to be received as comedy. Consider Cecil's report about the discovery of a new species of spider from episode 21, "A Memory of Europe":

> Big news in the science world! Scientists announce that they have discovered the world's deadliest spider: a previously unknown species that is as hard to spot as its bite is hard to survive. Apparently the specimen was found when your dead body was examined. They say you were a portrait of agony, your skin a myriad of pulsing, angry colors. Oh, you know what? I'm sorry. This report is from next week. Things have gotten so confusing ever since the wire services started using time machines. Never mind. No need to worry about that report for a few days. (Fink and Cranor, *Mostly Void* 213, 215)

There is some shock value at work, but because Cecil has a newsreader's trust from the listener, such an announcement is not of particular concern.

As circumstances draw Cecil closer to various events, his effect as a narrator changes. There are, for instance, cases where things happen to Cecil, but not on-air, or in real time with the listener present. These happen while the show is on the air, but we remain unimplicated in the events because Cecil, our filter, is still reporting and these things aren't happening directly to him right in the present moment; these tend to be occasion for subjective on-air reflection. In episode 29, "Subway," Cecil reports on the sudden installation of a subway system in Night Vale: The system has simply shown up over a series of days, with no records that one was ever planned. As the episode progresses and a great shaking from one of the nearby stops interrupts his broadcast, Cecil himself goes to investigate during the course of the weather segment. Up to this point, all of these reports are the third-person omniscient perspective expected of news reports. Following the weather segment, Cecil offers his own thoughts:

> It's spring somewhere, Night Vale, and I must admit the last few minutes—even stretched as they were seemingly into aeons—have left me feeling renewed, returned as I am to my home after so long away. It's like I'm walking into fresh, clean water, even as I lean into the mic.
>
> I entered the subway, like many of you, and like many of you other riders, I saw and felt the cosmic suffering of millennia, was witness to eras of countless births and deaths and wars and discoveries and kisses and plagues and knives and cold empty void. I saw it all at once and I could not make sense of any of it, but I understood it fully, and it took years, Night Vale. (Fink and Cranor, *Great Glowing Coils* 38–39)

In this instance, Cecil has experienced whatever it is he's reporting, but because it happened off the air, he has had time to do some filtering. The temporal gap between Cecil and the events reassures listeners: Because the event was in the past, the listener is assured of Cecil's safety, and of the return of the one link between us and the world of Night Vale. Cecil here is very much the news "anchor" who tethers us to Night Vale and signals how we should respond; if he isn't concerned, then we shouldn't be either.

The closest and perhaps most disconcerting degree of separation between Cecil and the listener is when there is no temporal separation at all between events and Cecil's reporting of them; these are the events that happen to Cecil while he's on the air. Because there is no temporal narrative separation between Cecil and the event, there is no time for him to intellectualize what is happening, and these moments as a result tend to be more raw and to yield greater emotional impact. Often times the primary emotion conveyed in these instances is fear and, as a result, concern is elicited from listeners due to some subversion of Night Vale norms. For example, in episode 2, "Glow Cloud," a mysterious glowing cloud has taken to creeping across Night Vale, raining increasingly large dead animals as it goes. Any notion of incredible danger is repeatedly and casually dismissed, but during the last segment before the weather, as he is reporting the progress of the Glow Cloud, an ominous machinic music bed is introduced, Cecil's tone of voice shifts into a low, menacing drone, and the words and delivery suggest that the Glow Cloud—through Cecil—is now the one speaking. For the sake of illustrating this shift in tone, I have marked the period of possession in italics; where the drone grows more severe, I have bolded and set the remainder of the text in small caps for its increasing severity:

> The Sheriff's Secret Police have apparently taken to shouting questions at the Glow Cloud, trying to ascertain what exactly it wants. So far, the Glow Cloud has not answered. *The Glow Cloud does not need to converse with us. It does not feel as we tiny humans feel. It has no need for thoughts or feelings of love.* **The Glow Cloud simply is. All hail the mighty Glow Cloud. ALL HAIL.** (Fink and Cranor, *Mostly Void* 16–17)

But the possession lasts for less than a minute. We are then taken to the weather segment, and then immediately following the weather, Cecil returns saying, "Sorry, listeners. Not sure what happened in that earlier section of the broadcast. As in, I actually don't remember what happened. Tried to play back the tapes, but they're all blank and smell faintly of vanilla" (17). It is an unnerving moment to lose a listener's sole narrator, but in this case the moment does not last; we're allowed to flounder in a lonely universe devoid of the familiar narrator, but we're not left alone for long. The weather segment also allows for additional suspense—a device used throughout the series—but the consequences that follow are rarely grave.

The Glow Cloud incident, all things considered, is a fairly minor one, with few lasting implications. One of the more dramatic examples of how *Night Vale* elicits listener response through "real-time reporting" comes from the particularly unusual two-part episode, "The Sandstorm" (episodes 19A and 19B). What makes these two episodes unique is that there are two mirroring episodes: the Night Vale edition (19A) and the Desert Bluffs edition (19B). Desert Bluffs is a neighboring town that, prior to this episode, is occasionally mentioned by Cecil as inferior to Night Vale, but the listener has no reason to suspect that Cecil speaks of it so poorly for any other reason other than his own bias and perpetuating small-town rivalry. The two episodes follow the same basic structure: There is a sandstorm coming through the area, and when it hits, duplicates of everyone seem to appear. Midway through the episode, each host discovers a glowing vortex on their respective studio walls and decides to go through it. The other town's host comes to the microphone before going to the weather. The original host then returns, saying they met someone in the vortex—Cecil saying he met "a foul devil of a man," the Desert Bluffs radio host Kevin saying he's sure he met his double—and then closes the show.

The point at which the host goes through the vortex is unnerving for the listener, though to different degrees for each account of events. In the Night Vale edition, we exchange a familiar voice—Cecil—with an unfamiliar one—Kevin. Kevin, for his part, sounds about as confused as the listener. When observing the older equipment and darker walls, he questions whether he's somehow gone back in time. But for having no idea where he is, he seems to take it in stride: "You may not know me, nor I you, but we have this mic, and this voice, and your warm ears blossoming open to hear comforting secrets in the vibrations of a voice that pulse so deep into your body your heart relaxes for a time" (Fink and Cranor, *Mostly Void* 179). He does make some curious observations, noting that everything is "much drier than it should be," and fleetingly describes "this odd and bloodless desk"; and while unusual, this isn't entirely off-the-mark for something in Night Vale. There has been a temporary loss of Cecil, but Kevin is a fellow radio voice from Desert Bluffs, and thus far the listener has no reason to regard him—or Desert Bluffs—with any particular concern.

The Desert Bluffs edition of "The Sandstorm," however, is more unnerving. The listener becomes more accustomed to Kevin's chipper style of presentation—chipper to the point of being alternately overbearing and creepy—and hears our first of many references to StrexCorp: "Look around you. Strex. Look inside you. Strex. Go to sleep. Strex. Believe in a smiling god. Strexcorp: It is everything" (Fink and Cranor, *Mostly Void* 184). The frequent praise of the same corporation could raise some suspicion, but we do have some notion of how the episode will progress, as structurally the two are the same, and we fully expect Cecil to come to the microphone as Kevin goes through the vortex. But when he does, only his voice is familiar; his ensuing panic is not:

What is this studio? What is this damnable studio? Night Vale, I do not know if you can hear me. This is Cecil, and I do not know where I am. It is clearly a radio studio, but the walls are covered in blood, and instead of dials and buttons on the soundboard, there is just animal viscera, glistening under the green LED lights. ...

There is so much blood, it is seeping into my shoes. There are—oh, masters of us all, no—teeth scattered across the floor. The window into the control booth is shattered and there is a swath of skin and a fistful of long clumping hair hanging from a sharp glass point. I do not know if this is even Night Vale. (Fink and Cranor, *Mostly Void* 190)

This studio is something out of a nightmare and is particularly unnerving for the listener because it's unnerving for Cecil. Because he and the listener are experiencing the studio at the same time, Cecil has no time to act as a filter—either in his description or his reaction—and thus has no time to intellectualize or soften details. From the Night Vale edition, the listener knows Cecil returns to Night Vale, and that he has come from some "horrible place," but the listener also knows that the Night Vale notion of "horrible" can be different from what usually inspires the term as there is mass panic over street cleaning, Valentine's Day, and puppy infestations. And, by the time Cecil returns in part A, he has had time to process what happened. But to hear him experience the Desert Bluffs studio unfiltered, and to hear him so unnerved, is unnerving to the listener as well due to the immediacy of the connection and our intimacy with Cecil.

Thirteen episodes following "The Sandstorm" in "Yellow Helicopters," Cecil announces—uneasily and in a rather stilted manner—that StrexCorp, the oft-cited evil corporation in Desert Bluffs, has acquired the Night Vale community radio station (Fink and Cranor, *Great Glowing Coils* 69–70). This moment is significant as it initiates the StrexCorp story arc that governs year two of *Night Vale* and that culminates in the dramatic rebellion of Night Vale residents. It is also significant because it involves Cecil so directly as a character in his own story—one put in the difficult position of being hesitant or unable to report his feelings directly. Listeners are therefore called upon to reflect on their knowledge of and intimacy with Cecil to "read between the lines" of his reporting about StrexCorp. Indeed, much of the information from Strex is issued with the gratingly pseudo-positive spin used by Kevin throughout "The Sandstorm," and which often thinly veils ill intent and ruthless aggression, though that veil grows thinner as rebellion begins to crop up more frequently.

There are instances when Cecil himself resists and attempts to be more open and direct, but these moments are presented as perilous for Cecil; in episode 36, "Missing," for example, Cecil explains that he has to sneak onto the radio station roof and patch his phone into the tower to continue his broadcast, and he reflects on the definition and necessity of heroes, as well as his own role:

> I sometimes wish I could tell you more. But I cannot. I cannot tell you everything I think you should hear because it is boring. Or it is unnecessary. Or it is very necessary but unapproved. There are many reasons I cannot always tell you what I want to tell you, but the main reason is that you need to find it out for yourselves. ... I just report the news. I just arrange it. You figure it out. You learn from it. You take action. You create the meaning. It is all up to you. And given my current broadcasting situation, it may be up to you for a long time. (Fink and Cranor, *Great Glowing Coils* 113–14)

But these moments of resistance are followed by sharp correction that the listener familiar with Cecil and *Night Vale* recognizes as forced and insincere; the next episode (episode 37, "The Auction") begins with "First off, welcome back. Everything is fine. Nothing's happening, if you know what I mean. You shouldn't know what I mean. If you do know, you should forget. I'm not going to mention anything and you're not going to hear anything and both of us will fail to remember" (117).

But as resistance becomes greater, the correction becomes more severe, until what is supposed to be Night Vale's big stand against Strex in episode 46, "Parade Day," fails, and our familiar narrator is taken away for his insubordination. For a few episodes, he is replaced with Kevin and Lauren, the station's new program manager and a StrexCorp executive. These untrustworthy voices are unsettling not only because they present everything with painful positivity and in heavy euphemism—for instance, framing a forced labor effort as a "company picnic" (Fink and Cranor, *Great Glowing* 225)—but also because this is the closest that they and Strex have come to the listener. This is also the first time Cecil has been entirely absent, which increases the initial baseline dread of episode 47, "Company Picnic," that the events of that episode exacerbate. But then his absence makes his return all the greater, because once again we have a trustworthy and familiar voice to share with us the arc's climax and dénouement as Night Vale triumphs over the malevolent StrexCorp.

The voice of Night Vale is finally more than a voice. Cecil is a presence conjured into being through a collaboration with the listener. As he slips from objective reporter to the first-person narrator, intimacy is established and Cecil moves beyond being merely a conduit for information about a small desert town to become a curious kind of friend with whom we can't speak or interact, but about whom we care nevertheless. Our affective engagement with Cecil is then amplified by both the immediacy of sound in general and the "real-time" reporting of dramatic events. As Cecil shifts from objective reporter to subjective commentator to the first-person narrator, he increasingly involves us in his life, testifying to the power of voice to create a sense of intimacy, immediacy, and presence.

Works Cited

Davis, Eleanor. "Who Needs Friends When You've Got Terry Gross?" *The New Yorker*, 25 March 2014. www.newyorker.com/culture/culture-desk/who-needs-friends-when-youve-got-terry-gross.

Fink, Joseph, and Jeffrey Cranor. *The Great Glowing Coils of the Universe: Welcome to Night Vale Episodes, Volume 2*. Harper Perennial, 2016a.

———. *Mostly Void, Partially Stars: Welcome to Night Vale Episodes, Volume 1*. Harper Perennial, 2016b.

Granly, Erik. "Acousmatic Space: Ann Lislegaard's Sound Projects." *Ann Lislegaard: Science Fiction and Other Worlds*. Astrup Fearnley Museum of Modern Art, 2007. Accessed February 5, 2018. lislegaard.com/?p=328.

Green, Melanie C., Jeffrey J. Strange, and Timothy C. Brock, eds. *Narrative Impact: Social and Cognitive Foundations*. Lawrence Erlbaum, 2002.

Nancy, Jean-Luc. *Listening*. Trans. Charlotte Mandell. Fordham University Press, 2007.

Oatley, Keith. "Emotions and the Story Worlds of Fiction." In *Narrative Impact: Social and Cognitive Foundations*, ed. M.C. Green, J.J. Strange, and T.C. Brock, 39–69. Lawrence Erlbaum, 2002.

Peralta, Eyder. "After 5-Decade Career, NPR's Carl Kasell Will Retire." *NPR. National Public Radio*, 4 March 2014. www.npr.org/sections/thetwo-way/2014/03/04/285780588/after-five-decade-career-nprs-carl-kasell-will-retire.

Polichak, James W., and Richard J. Gerrig. "'Get Up and Win!': Participatory Responses to Narrative." In *Narrative Impact: Social and Cognitive Foundations*, ed. M.C. Green, J.J. Strange, and T.C. Brock, 71–95. Lawrence Erlbaum, 2002.

Verma, Neil. *Theater of the Mind: Imagination, Aesthetics, and American Radio Drama*. University of Chicago Press, 2012.

CHAPTER 7

Who Killed Cecil Palmer? The Role of Memory in *Night Vale*'s Self-Narrative Rupture

Michael Patrick Vaughn

Abstract How does Cecil know who he is if he cannot remember who he was? Using the *Welcome to Night Vale* episode "Cassette" as a jumping-off point, I argue that Cecil draws upon an array of mnemonic practices to cope with his forgotten past and a forced remembering of what appears to be a violent moment in his childhood. Cecil copes with the trauma of forced remembering by deciding that he will forget again until he feels prepared to remember again. Cecil's journey to remember and forget serves as a case to understand individual agency in shaping one's own self-narrative via remembering and forgetting. I close with a discussion of theoretical implications for both sudden, individual-level trauma and the study of memory broadly.

Keywords Cassette • Cecil • Forgetting • Memory • Narrative • Self • The Man in the Tan Jacket

M. P. Vaughn (✉)
Sociology Department, Emory University, Atlanta, GA, USA
e-mail: michael.patrick.vaughn@emory.edu

J. A. Weinstock (ed.), *Critical Approaches to* Welcome to Night Vale,
https://doi.org/10.1007/978-3-319-93091-6_7

> *And I came across these cassette tapes marked "Cecil Radio Test. Age 15." You know, listeners, I have no memory whatsoever of making these tapes. Isn't that so weird? At one point they must have meant so much to me, and* now they are just objects, with no remembered life attached to them. *(Episode 33, "Cassette," emphasis added)*

How do we integrate newly discovered moments from our past into how we see ourselves? Cecil Gershwin Palmer, The Voice of Night Vale, does so by enacting a live editing of his past to actively create and maintain a consistent self-narrative.[1] Cecil cannot remember much of his childhood. Listeners learn about these gaps in Cecil's biography as he discovers them himself, through discarded cassette tapes, the near-homecoming of long-lost friends, now ghosts, and the mysterious auction of Lot 37.[2] For the listener, as for Cecil, the mysterious cassettes simultaneously disrupt and make continuous Cecil's biography; they provide narratives to fill in the gaps they expose. And yet Cecil presents himself as *already having a consistent biography.* This presentation could be contrasted with the case of The Man in the Tan Jacket, as he passively is forgotten by others and Cecil actively forgets himself. Sociologists often conceptualize the self, who we are, as a collection of social roles bound together by one's own memory (Mead); if an individual cannot recall that they were once, say, a radio station intern, those experiences and that role do not factor into one's understanding of their own self, even though others may and do recall. How, then, can Cecil make claims to having a consistent sense of self, having *always been,* given this apparent rupture in his biography? And what can this tell us about how people generally retain a sense of selfhood in the face of disconfirming, potentially traumatic experiences?

Using Cecil as a case, I argue that individuals defend their self-narrative, the story of who they are, from disruption and rupture *despite evidence to the contrary.* This is done using an array of mnemonic devices, enacted until a time when they can regain control and maintain potentially new-found, narrative consistency. To demonstrate this, I will first briefly describe the city of Night Vale and the unique qualities of Night Valian memory. I will then discuss the case of Troy Walsh and The Man in the Tan Jacket, focusing on violations of role expectations and mass forgetting. Then, I will describe the case of Cecil Gershwin Palmer, who is unable to recall large chunks of his past, framing my discussion primarily around the episode "Cassette" (episode 33). I will analyze these cases using sociological conceptualizations of self and collective memory to provide a theoretical frame of and mechanistic account for what occurs in the podcast. I argue that Cecil deploys a number of mnemonic tactics—both continuity practices, which collapse timelines, and discontinuity practices, which divide them, to preserve the consistency of his self-narrative. I will close this chapter with a discussion of how these self-maintenance processes outlined have real-world implications, emphasizing the inherently active nature of memory and selfhood. Individuals have the capacity to, and actively do, shape their own self through the use of continuity and discontinuity practices. The individual's ability to actively edit their own biography allows for the individual to integrate (or reject) new self-relevant information and shape/maintain their self-narrative. This process, in part, shapes how we remember ourselves, which shapes *who we are* in the social world.

Cecil often forgets or misremembers events in his daily life. Part of the reason for this is a stratagem of the Vague Yet Menacing Government Agency to maintain control of Night Vale. The City Council regularly threatens "re-education" against those who are too aware of the government (see, e.g., episode 7, "History Week"; episode 28, "Summer Reading Program"), instituting the offense of thought crime (episode 9, "PYRAMID"), and even banning writing utensils to control the flow of information (episode 8, "The Lights in Radon Canyon"). The City Council also for a long time had an outright ban on the discussion of angels, despite their visibility and the support they provide to the city throughout Old Woman Josie's life (episode 97, "Josephina") and during the battle with StrexCorp (episode 49, "Old Oak Doors" parts A and B), which caused Cecil and fellow Night Valians to outwardly deny their existence. But this was more often than not a matter of lip service, saying what the Sheriff's Secret Police wanted to hear from an unmarked van outside your house, rather than a statement of actual belief.

In addition to being forced to feign forgetting unsanctioned thoughts through vicious thought crime legislation, the citizens of Night Vale seem to have generally developed a coping strategy of *actually forgetting* that which is too distressing or does not fit into their already-weirder-than-typical world view. The case of The Man in the Tan Jacket epitomizes what is unthinkable for Night Valians, largely because he himself became unthinkable due to such a world view violation. When Troy Walsh commits the taboo of leaving Night Vale to move to King City, The Man in the Tan Jacket, King City's mayor, becomes perpetually forgotten. Troy leaves Night Vale for complicated personal and familial reasons, mostly centered around heartbreak and loss regarding his children (Josh and Jackie) and former sweetheart (Diane). By leaving Night Vale, Troy does the unthinkable; he abandons his home and violates his role as father, partner, and resident. It is because of this role violation, this interpersonal insult, that mass amnesia ensues. The entirety of *Welcome to Night Vale: A Novel* is premised upon resolving this insult, ultimately through Troy returning to Night Vale, and both The Man in the Tan Jacket and Troy attempting to resume the roles they had previously abandoned. We, the audience, learn that The Man in the Tan Jacket ultimately can be remembered (episode 76, "Epilogue"), implying that resuming one's place in the world has the capacity to right this mnemonic wrong.

Memory, in the case of The Man in the Tan Jacket, becomes a dysfunctional coping mechanism for both The Man in the Tan Jacket and Troy Walsh. Troy was faced with a situation with which he could not cope: He was a romantic partner and father "born with the ability to be all things to all people but nothing to any one person" (Fink and Cranor, *Welcome to Night Vale: A Novel* 383). Troy was unable to fulfill two of his social roles, pieces of his self, and chose to flee. By taking control and fleeing, and through the weirdness of Night Vale, he infected King City, causing The Man in the Tan Jacket, who similarly was not fulfilling his roles of husband or father, to be forgotten. In both the case of The Man in the Tan Jacket and Troy, these men found pieces of themselves incredibly distressing, being unable to support others (e.g., children, partner, family, city) and fled. Troy literally fled. The Man in the Tan Jacket was erased.

Cecil Palmer juxtaposes The Man in the Tan Jacket and Troy in that he neither literally flees nor is he passively forgotten. Cecil is agentic in the shaping of his present through an active shaping of his self-narrative, a means of defensively, perhaps dysfunctionally protecting the continuity of who he is. In "The Shape in Grove Park" (episode 5), Cecil has what appears to be a small existential crisis, concerned that he is "literally the only person in the world, speaking to [himself] in a fit of madness caused by [his] inability to admit the tragedy of [his] own existence" (Fink and Cranor, *Mostly Void* 45). This crisis is at least partially fueled by Cecil's inherent doubt in his own memory and perception—"Is it possible that I only imagined [Intern] Leland, and forgot making myself this cup of coffee?" (*Mostly Void* 45). In "Faceless Old Woman" (episode 26), Cecil remembers very few aspects of his mother, such as her prediction about his death: "Someone's going to kill you one day, Cecil, and it will involve a mirror. Mark my words, child" (Fink and Cranor, *Great Glowing Coils* 7). Most of his past, however, is unclear and unspoken.

And yet Cecil continues to be Cecil. Whereas Troy took on countless additional roles and occupations to escape inconsistency in his self-narrative, being a father who cannot father, and The Man in the Tan Jacket was entirely forgotten for his inadequacy to father or to mayor, Cecil continues to be The Voice of Night Vale. Sociological theories of self tend to position memory as the force that allows for the disparate social roles one holds (e.g., son, radio host, Night Vale citizen) to cohere and remain a unified self (Cecil as consistently Cecil). Social interaction and one's subsequent experiential memories allow for the maintenance of self by giving us a sense of who we were, which we can compare to who we are and thus identify change and consistency. This change signals discontinuity, becoming something different, and consistency signal continuity, having always have been the same. The assumption built into this conceptualization of self and memory is a desire of consistency; individuals seek to avoid ruptures in their self-narrative and generally remain the same person (e.g., Teenage Cecil and Adult Cecil are still both Cecil, despite their different developmental stages and periods of existence).

In "Cassette" (episode 33), we, the audience, are given a glimpse into how Cecil manages this consistency of self, given an otherwise inconsistent biography. Cecil experiences a rupture in his self-narrative when he finds a collection of tapes from his childhood titled "Cecil Radio Test. Age 15." These tapes were presumably recorded by Cecil as a teenager, recounting some of his daily life and excitement at the prospect of being on the radio one day. Cecil is brought to stunned silence by these tapes; he does not remember recording them, nor their content.

In these tapes, Cecil learns he had a brother and about the start of his career in radio, followed by what sounds like the fulfillment of his mother's prophecy regarding his own death. The tapes "don't make sense" to Cecil; what he hears is incompatible with his own remembered biography. The apparent sound of his mother's prophecy coming to fruition, of the murder of Teenage Cecil in front of the hall mirror, is so incompatible with his own remembrance, his own self-narrative, that Cecil destroys the tape and vows that this instance will be forgotten.

[(Teenage Cecil) *screams. There is gurgling. A body falls to the floor. Tape hiss continues. The tape shuts off. End Teenage voice.*]
     What is this? What is this?

> What...
>
> No matter! I'm taking the tape, just now and I'm [*Grunts*] crushing it into little pieces. None of us have to think about it again. I'll just double check that the mirror in the station bathroom is covered as usual and then that will be that. Done. Forgotten. (Fink and Cranor, *Great Glowing Coils* 81)

Cecil rejects this narrative and destroys the only record of it, claiming he will forget it, has forgotten it, destroyed any bridge between then and now. In a stark departure from his overt treatment of the existence of angels, Cecil does not deny that this event ever occurred; instead, Cecil simply decides to forget it. If he were to remember the contents of the cassette, the way he understood himself would have to change (e.g., intern, brother, potentially a childhood victim of assault). These new roles would be incorporated into his self-narrative. By actively forgetting, Cecil allows himself to preserve his biography as it was; the narrative he held before the cassettes played still defines who he is. I call this an *active* forgetting because, unlike The Man in the Tan Jacket, Cecil must expend effort to control the spread of this narrative (i.e., destroying the tape) and states that this new information will be forgotten. This active forgetting extends beyond denial, almost into a form of dissociation, rejecting the notion that The Voice of Teenage Cecil could ever have been the same person as The Voice of Night Vale.

The act of destroying the cassettes is an act of self-maintenance. Cecil does not recall interning at the radio station nor does he remember anything about the previous host, Leonard Burton, or even what happened to his brother (episode 56, "Cassette"). This lack of memory, paired with the implication of violent trauma, spurred Cecil to destroy the tape, thus destroying the only record of this inconsistency. Though others *do* remember Cecil's youth, as shown by Lucia's recounting of Cecil's little league baseball performance (episode 84, "Past Time") and the presumed fact that others heard Cecil play the tapes, destroying the cassettes leaves no physical record, or relic, that can contradict Cecil's biography. Equally as important as Cecil destroying the tape, though, is his declaration that the event is "Forgotten." The act of destruction is paired with the act of forgetting. Cecil is actively managing what he chooses to remember and incorporate into his self-narrative. To better understand how Cecil could actively forget and how it might protect the consistency of his biography, and thus allow for self-maintenance, I draw on mnemonic mechanisms outlined in the field of collective memory.

Collective memories, sitting at the intersection of culture and social psychology, are shared cognition across social groups or societies (Halbwachs). Collective memories tend to be group-relevant and to be roughly similar across all group members, including those who did not directly experience the event, such as Night Valians' shared remembrance of the terror of Street Cleaning Day (episode 15, "Street Cleaning Day"). Collective memories provide individuals with a shared understanding of the nature of their group. Zerubavel describes human memory as inherently social, something that, "while far from being absolutely objective, nonetheless transcends our own subjectivity and is shared by others around us" (*Hidden Rhythm* 81). These memories, regardless of their group orientation, are still remembered by individuals. To put it another way, collective memories are conceived of as group- or societal-level phenomena that occur within the individual's minds.[3]

By this logic, all groups have some form of collective memory, becoming collective in nature only through a perceived consensus about the past. This could be an origin story, such as illegal knowledge of the founding of Night Vale (episode 7, "History Week"), a shared tradition (e.g., bloodstone circles), or any folkway (e.g., paying homage to the almighty Glow Cloud—all hail). Collective memory situates group membership within a shared history, a history which is encoded as memories which the individual may not have directly experienced. The cassettes act as a disruption of collective memory for Cecil. By informing him that he has held additional roles which he cannot recall (brother and intern), the cassettes not only impact his perception of his self, but they also call into question his own access to the collective memories of these groups (family, radio station, city of Night Vale). If his recollection does not match that of others', then his memories may not be collective memories. This disruption leaves Cecil to deal with a new continuity (his radio career extending throughout much of his adolescence) and a new source of discontinuity (a time before and after the disappearance of his brother) in his self-narrative.

In keeping with theories of collective memory, I argue that Cecil enacts continuity and discontinuity practices to manage these ruptures. Historical continuity is the perception that a group or society has remained the same over time, collapsing different iterations within different social contexts into one broad identity (see Zerubavel, *Time Maps*). Historical discontinuity is the division of a group's timeline into discrete periods, using events or time periods to denote different group identities. As Zerubavel writes, "not only do we attribute to an entire historical 'period' a single, uniform identity, we also attribute separate identities to what we consider 'separate' periods" (*Time Maps* 87). From this frame, we can imagine Night Vale as both always having been Night Vale (continuous) and also being different Night Vales at different points in time (e.g., city government under Mayors Winchell and Cardinal; before and after Carlos' arrival; Night Vale Community Radio under Leonard Berton and Cecil Palmer).

Continuity and discontinuity are generally co-occurring practices. A group that divides its biography into discrete periods (via discontinuity practices) must also maintain uniformity within each period by using continuity. Individual Night Valians appear to simultaneously divide their governance between the reign of Pamela Winchell and Dana Cardinal while also holding that each piece was one coherent reign, meaning that while Mayor Winchell was mayor, she was always and consistently mayor. This co-occurrence appears facile to state but is vital to think through histories and narratives; without both continuity and discontinuity, narratives could only be all or nothing, either everything occurred within one timeline or events become entirely subdivided. We would discuss Night Vale Community Radio either as a series of subdivided broadcasts or as one long history spanning multiple radio hosts with little in-between.

In this way, most historical narratives are (dis)continuous, meaning they rely on both continuity and discontinuity. Cecil's self-narrative is put in jeopardy by the cassettes because he is confronted with evidence that challenges his biography, thus challenging his claims to a consistent self-narrative. In terms of his radio career, Cecil's discontinuous narrative—that he was once not in radio and now he is—is ruptured with evidence of his internship and long-standing love of radio. His continuous narrative about family, having one mother and a relatively non-violent childhood, is also ruptured by what sounds like a violent attack. This new evidence challenges Cecil's biography, the story he holds about his own biography. Evidence that one's previously held (dis)continuous biography may be inaccurate challenges one's claim to a consistent self-narrative, thus impacting how the individual understands their self in a very real and immediate way. Cecil is so panic-stricken by this revelation that he is nearly speechless. Cecil's response to the cassette, it would follow, is not exclusively a rejection of a history that is incongruous with his self-narrative, but also a result of the friction between his desire for a cohesive self (to understand one's self fully, through one's memory of one's social roles) and for a consistent self-narrative (to retain the same biography while accruing new experiences). Cecil quells this friction by utilizing both continuity and discontinuity practices.

Historical continuity can be socially created through constancy of place, access to relics and memorabilia, imitation and replication of the past, historical analogy, language use, and overlap of past and present (see Zerubavel, *Time Maps* 40–54). Consistency of place is achieved if the physical location remains constant (e.g., Cecil has always lived in Night Vale and the radio station has always existed). This consistency would support his narrative of being The Voice of Night Vale, a valued role for Cecil. However, continuity practices may also challenge other valued roles, thus challenging Cecil's self-narrative. The cassettes themselves function as relics, bridging the past and present. These physical objects act as "mnemonic bridges" which function as "*tangible* links between past and present selves" (*Time Maps* 45). For Cecil, bringing the past to the present impacts how he understands himself as a radio host (having no memory of being an intern), as a member of a family (having no memory of being a brother), and as a child (having no memory of the implied attack). All of these factors weaken Cecil's claim to a consistent self-narrative. Cecil attempts to circumvent this continuity by preventing any fusion of the past and present through the destruction of the tape; by destroying this narrative-violating relic, Cecil prevents the past from holding tangible space in the present and thereby prevents the past from impacting his present self. With no memory of the event and a refusal of the narrative, by explicitly narrating to his listeners that this event is "Forgotten," Cecil metaphorically burns that mnemonic bridge.

Discontinuity allows for social groups to create historical eras, through periodization, emphasizing or creating divisions to signal change or difference. Cecil, interestingly, never rejects the reality of the cassettes. He does not create social distance, claiming one iteration of Cecil evolved from a previous iteration, or argue that Teenage Cecil resided in a different time period, dividing past and present at an arbitrary cut point. Cecil decides to actively forget, to remove these memories forcibly, to disassociate and destroy any relic to protect his self-narrative. His forcible removal of any connection to the past found on those cassettes is known as mnemonic cutting. Mnemonic cutting is a discontinuity practice in which the actor intentionally creates a rupture in the biography. Cecil, however, utilizes this discontinuity practice to enact narrative continuity. He excises these memories not to periodize, as one would expect when using discontinuous practices. Instead, Cecil is creating a rupture, an absence, a void in his biography in order to maintain the illusion of sameness. Cecil has not divided his life into before and after the attack in the mirror (periodization and discontinuity) or incorporated it as just one piece of larger biography (mnemonic bridging and continuity); he has created a chiasmus in which discontinuous practices create the illusion of continuity of self-narrative.

How, then, can we explain this case? Cecil goes to extensive lengths to maintain and control the apparent consistency of his self-narrative. By actively forgetting the contents of the cassettes, through their physical destruction and great mnemonic work, Cecil is able to successfully avoid immediate integration of these events into his biography, which would force him to adjust his self-narrative and undergo the potentially traumatic experience of re-evaluating who he is. The problem with this resolution is that it excludes the rest of the social world; the cassette has been destroyed and forgotten, but all of Night Vale heard its contents and have access to this narrative. I argue that the act of denying history functions differently than re-packaging it. Cecil is attempting to make a continuity argument, that things have always been the same in his life, while employing discontinuity practices, such as mnemonic cutting. This creates another paradox, one of sameness despite rupture. To return to his previously held self-narrative, Cecil enacts discontinuity practices (mnemonic cutting) to excise the aspects of his lived reality which have been introduced via the cassette. By destroying the relic (the cassettes) and choosing to forget the narrative, Cecil can create an "actual historical gap" (Zerubavel, *Time Maps* 82). But this gap is surrounded by sameness—his previously continuous history remains intact, allowing him to experience his self as consistent once again.

Once Cecil destroyed the tape, he not only re-created his historical continuity and consistency, he also effectively regained control over his self by determining which roles he would acknowledge and which will be forgotten. Given the trauma of "Cassette," Cecil desires control over his own self-narrative. When these circumstances are viewed within the context of the hostile takeover of Night Vale Community Radio by StrexCorp, which reduced his autonomy as a radio host and also left him financially in jeopardy, being paid only in StrexCorp credit (episode 37, "The Auction"), control becomes paramount for Cecil. This distinction comes through in Cecil's different descriptions of the cassettes (episode 33) and Lot 37 (episode 37); Cecil initially introduces the cassettes with a naïve excitement, whereas Cecil is clearly afraid when he describes Lot 37. Cecil's reaction to Lot 37, just as it was after he listened to the cassettes, is to control this new relic that could endanger the consistency of his self-narrative. After framing Lot 37 as something that "is of a certain interest to [him]," Cecil quickly becomes more and more candid about the gravity of the auction, explaining that "if I did not win Lot 37 I would be unraveled. Perhaps I would be unraveled either way" (Fink and Cranor, *Great Glowing* 123). The unraveling he fears here is also the unraveling the listeners hear during "Cassette," the unraveling of his self-narrative. After losing the bid for Lot 37, Cecil closes his broadcast with the following:

> Listeners, accumulating objects is just a way, we hope, *to turn back the grim specter of death*. Thank you for your participation in this auction, and for your hope that making a certain purchase—All-Clad cookware, a candelabrum, a comic book, a community radio show host—would render you any more than mortal.
>
> I go now to find myself, or to find who has myself, or to find someone that might make me feel better about what has happened today. I'd take that last one, honestly. I'd take that honest last one. (*Great Glowing* 124; emphasis added)

Cecil sees Lot 37 as an opportunity to *feel better* about himself more so than a way to *find himself*. It is also a way to avoid the metaphorical "death" of his current self. By losing the auction bid, Cecil is unable to gain possession of Lot 37, stripping him of his ability to enact mnemonic practices and continue to (re)shape his self-narrative.

Homecoming was another such moment when Cecil was presented with an opportunity to learn more about his past and actively manage his self-narrative. Homecoming in Night Vale functions like a massive séance, in which "all of the Night Vale High alumni come together ... current students, former students, students long dead, future students who aren't born yet" (episode 56, "Homecoming"). This is the first instance where Cecil directly refers to "those old cassette tapes" and the "important questions" they raised for him. Cecil hopes to use homecoming as an opportunity to talk to his mother to learn more about his past, on his own terms. The event is eventually canceled, due to the questionable existence of the Night Vale Scorpions' running back, meaning Cecil is again thwarted in his attempt to actively seek out information about his past. By retaining ignorance until information is available, Cecil continues to control his self-narrative even in his failings.

Cecil's live editing of his own biography functions as a case study in the inherently active nature of both memory and selfhood. Memory is typically conceptualized at the individual level and sociologically trapped as experiential and interactional, meaning one can only remember what one has perceived or done. Collective memory scholars provide a route to escape this narrow frame by re-conceptualizing memory as broadly social, centering the focus on groups and societies by outlining mechanisms through which these entities can create their own histories. My contribution to this discussion is the bridging of individual-level and societal-level conceptualizations of memory. I argue that the self is actively maintained when an individual manages their self-narrative. The individual has agency over their biography, which will influence not only what they remember about their self but more importantly who they are. Cecil's use of continuity and discontinuity practices, and by implication, his ability to excise painful memories and, when ready, slowly approach alternative sources of self-information, demonstrate one such way this could occur.

We as listeners and scholars and fans can take away much from this array of self-maintenance tactics, most especially a deeper understanding of how we cope with new information about who we are and who we have been. The return of Cecil's past, through the cassettes, is traumatic; it shakes him to even entertain the idea of having lived through such a different, violent past. While not all biographical ruptures are violent, the realization that one was not quite who they expected to be can be traumatic. Using Cecil as a case study, we can see that people have the capacity to be highly creative in how they protect themselves, stalling for time while they find ways to address (or prevent) the changes in their self-narrative. The foils I present, Troy Walsh and The Man in the Tan Jacket, pose a further question about the nature of selfhood: is consistency of self-narrative always necessary? While Cecil frames his self-maintenance around consistency and control, Troy and The Man in the Tan Jacket actually end up resolving their stories through an alteration of self-narrative, an acknowledgment of loss and change. I would argue that selfhood may be defensively rooted in maintenance and stasis, but this is neither the default nor the most useful practice. The malleability of one's own memory, especially given its relationship to the memory of individual others' and the collective, may provide additional mechanistic accounts for self-maintenance and, potentially, (re)formation.

NOTES

1. In the following chapter, I focus on the impact of history on current self. This primarily includes events which either have occurred and are integrated into the self (Cecil was hired as a radio host and knows this) or those which are forgotten (Cecil has no recollection of having a brother). Events which occur in the present are also subject to the same set of mnemonic practices, either being commemorated or forgotten, but they are outside of the domain of the present discussion.
2. I use "biography" and "self-narrative" interchangeably, referring to the story an individual internalizes about who they are. This story is rooted in events that have occurred in the past.
3. For more information about the sociological interplay between group- and individual-level phenomena, see Coleman.

WORKS CITED

Coleman, James S. *Foundations of Social Theory.* Harvard University Press, 1990.

Fink, Joseph, and Jeffrey Cranor. *Welcome to Night Vale: A Novel.* Harper Perennial, 2015.

——. *The Great Glowing Coils of the Universe: Welcome to Night Vale Episodes, Volume 2.* Harper Perennial, 2016a.

——. *Mostly Void, Partially Stars: Welcome to Night Vale Episodes, Volume 1.* Harper Perennial, 2016b.

Halbwachs, Maurice. *On Collective Memory.* Ed. Lewis A. Coser. The University of Chicago Press, 1992.

Mead, George Herbert. *Mind, Self, & Society.* The University of Chicago Press, 1934.

Zerubavel, Eviatar. *Hidden Rhythms: Schedules and Calendars in Social Life.* The University of Chicago Press, 1981.

——. *Time Maps: Collective Memory and the Social Shape of the Past.* The University of Chicago Press, 2003.

CHAPTER 8

Ode for the Lights Above the Arby's: Reading *Welcome to Night Vale* Through the Lens of Poetry

Elliott Freeman

Abstract This chapter examines the poetics of *Night Vale*—the manifold ways in which it uses poetic forms, style, and diction to subvert expectation and mark passage into the liminal world of poetic thought. These "intrusions" disorient the listener, rejuvenating the show's trademark strangeness. Through diverse forms and strategies, from the bastardized haikus that open each episode to the powerful sense of lineation that defines the host's staccato delivery, *Night Vale* draws on the inherent unfamiliarity of poetry to place breath, motion, and tension at the forefront of the audience's experience. In this way, the language of poetry becomes the language of oddity, a defining feature and indispensable tool for creating and maintaining uncertainty.

Keywords Language • Poetry • Rhythm • Uncertainty

E. Freeman (✉)
Jefferson College of Health Sciences, Roanoke, VA, USA

© The Author(s) 2018
J. A. Weinstock (ed.), *Critical Approaches to* Welcome to Night Vale,
https://doi.org/10.1007/978-3-319-93091-6_8

Welcome to Night Vale is joyously, self-avowedly strange; it revels in surreal departures from reality and resistance to normalcy. That strangeness is, in fact, one of the primary pleasures of *Night Vale* (the podcast, not the un-italicized desert town); like a good joke, it works to subvert our expectations. According to co-creator Joseph Fink in *Mostly Void, Partially Stars*, one of the podcast's goals has always been "to make the mundane terrifying, and the terrifying mundane" (131). Safe to say that it succeeds in this mission—in the surreal desertscape of Night Vale, librarians are transformed into child-stealing monsters and the banality of street-cleaning day is reimagined as a hellish ordeal reminiscent of 1950s atomic jitters. In describing *Night Vale*, it's easy to attribute its bizarre élan to content alone, but this overlooks the ways in which the podcast's craft leverages poetic techniques—especially its keen sense of rhythm and tension—to keep the audience off balance, leaving them receptive to an alternative to reality full of secret police, smiling gods, and floating cats.

Poetry is notoriously difficult to pin down. There are as many definitions as there are poets, critics, fans, and textbooks, ranging from "memorable speech" (Auden, as qtd. in Firchow 30) to "language at its most distilled and powerful" ("Rita Dove"). Trying to articulate a coherent definition with rigorous inclusion and exclusion criteria is a proverbial windmill. And yet, if presented with a text, most readers will have an instinctual response to the question: "Is this poetry?" A gut reaction would likely say that, no, *Welcome to Night Vale* is obviously not poetry, especially as the genre is popularly understood—a baffling assemblage of words on a page. Despite this, *Night Vale* clearly shares many of poetry's core concerns with structural, syntactical, linguistic, rhythmic, and even performative features.

We might then read *Night Vale* as "poetic," but there are few other adjectives so deeply abused. To many people, "poetic" is a versatile, gauzy description, something meant to describe romance and beauty—or, less charitably, something precious and pointless. Regardless, it is not difficult to regard *Night Vale* as poetic in its construction—not actually intended to be read poetry, but so closely aligned that the distinction is rendered (mostly) unimportant. The podcast is at its most poem-like when it tightens and quickens its language, leveraging repetition, rhythm, and enjambment; this is evident in the opening and closing to each episode, and doubly so in *Night Vale*'s eccentric advertisements. Throughout its performance and delivery, it is saturated in the tropes of poetic performance, with the calculated cadence and careful pauses of a modern reading. It also partakes of poetry's obsession with language *as* language, not just a vessel for the transmission of narrative but a device beautiful in and of itself, whether rendered in lush extravagance or austerity. And, while a far cry from the precise meter of classical poets, *Night Vale* nonetheless maintains a sense of modulated rhythm throughout, an erratic tension between stressed and unstressed. This is particularly important because, as one of a few key features to most poetry, meter is an aural phenomenon, not a visual one (Orr). Small wonder that even irregular rhythm can impart a sense of poetry.

There is a certain degree of hubris involved in unilaterally claiming that something is poetry (or poetic, or poem-like). Poetry might resist easy definition, but it's reasonable to assert that authorial intention should play a role: A poem is something written by a poet with the intention of *being* a poem. Of *Night Vale*'s creators, Joseph Fink has published a poem in 2014 ("Let Me Tell You About New York City"), but that was well into the podcast's run. Co-creator Jeffrey Cranor features a number of pre-*Night Vale* poems on his personal website, but both Cranor and Fink describe themselves and their work in terms of drama and theater, not poetry.

Why, then, should poetry matter for critical audiences of *Welcome to Night Vale*? Because poetry *intrudes*, and that intrusion is key to the show's aesthetics. Every aspect of *Night Vale* is calibrated to unsettle, either subtly or directly, by transforming the mundane into the surreal. Fictional host Cecil Palmer (voiced by less-fictional actor, Cecil Baldwin) delivers his eerily intimate broadcasts with unnatural emphasis, pronouncing words with surgical care and leaving pauses that provoke uncertainty in the listener. While his performance is markedly different from the crisp, prim readings of poets like Edna St. Vincent Millay who made space for their art in the nascence of broadcast radio, both share a sense of the uncanny—that these voices are more sensitive, more sensual than those we expect to find on the radio. Poetry is commonly misunderstood as intensely personal, but there *is* something intensely poetic about intimacy. In her own readings, Millay "seems to have understood the irony of disembodied voice: a radio reading ... brings the poet closer to the audience than when she recites her work in a crowded hall" (Wheeler 55). That *Night Vale* draws on its framing device to bring Cecil and listener into close proximity only furthers its appearance as a hybrid object—not a poem itself, but a not-so-distant cousin.

We certainly do not have the immediate indicators of poetry in *Welcome to Night Vale*—both of the current transcript collections render scripts as pure and uncomplicated prose, with no hint of "the ragged right edges and arbitrary lines" that many associate as the core signifiers of a poem (Yakich). Turning to the *intention* of poetry though, there is a common idea that "a poem still has the ability to surprise" (Yakich) and "purges from our inward sight the film of familiarity which obscure from us the wonder of our being" (Shelley). If prose is defined by unity of time, place, and causality, then poetry is universal, atemporal—and at its weirdest and most poem-like, *Night Vale* bobs up from the steady current of its narrative and concerns itself with images divorced from any strict timeframe, even if those images are just the haunting lights above the Arby's that signify some impending peril.

Every episode of *Welcome to Night Vale* opens and closes with the podcast's keenest and closest foray into traditional poetry. Greeting the audience, our host Cecil Palmer offers up the bastard child of haiku and aphorism, something sharp, pointed, and (usually) entirely unrelated to the episode at large. Each introduction is workmanlike in its careful construction, densely packed with concrete imagery and set to a clear rhythm reminiscent of the haiku's traditional sets of five, seven, and five syllables, although not bound to any precise measurements.

Consider "Subway" (episode 29) and its cold open: "Our black suns move erratically, like drunken bees, and each of them stings. Now more than ever we are full of blood and honey." Read as strictly transcribed prose, it loses a great deal of its power precisely because that power is bound up in Palmer's choice of pauses. If we choose instead to transcribe these sentences to preserve their poem-like nature, we might instead render it as "Our black suns // move / erratically, // like drunken bees // and each of them / stings. Now more than ever / we are full / of blood // and honey." This better reflects the pauses in this short passage, both great (indicated by a "//," usually reserved for stanza breaks in poetry) and small (indicated by "/," standing in for a line break). Although this transcription is hardly definitive—Palmer pauses between "black" and "suns" just long enough that it could be read as a line break instead—it nonetheless reveals how much meaning and rhythm is stripped away when *Welcome to Night Vale* is read as prose rather than as verse, or at least as a chimera of the two.

In particular, it is important to note the second sentence, lineated in this reading as a tercet and then a one-line stanza. That hanging orphan, "and honey," is an exemplar for the alchemy of the line break in poetry: In the half-second of silence between the two, the audience is held, suspended, between one possible conclusion and another. To say that they are now full of blood and honey recasts the metaphor of the suns-as-bees, offering up the possibility that, at least in the dreamscape logic of Night Vale, the line between metaphor and reality may be uncomfortably hazy. More tellingly, this draws on the poetic turn, the device by which a poet suspends meaning, often at a line or stanza break, to draw out and juxtapose one potential reading against another. Present in poetry across the world and the centuries, these turns are one of the foremost powers of verse, revealing the inherent ambiguity of language by forcing a phrase to be read both within and without its context. Like the volta of a sonnet, which comes at the end to dramatically recast everything that has come before it, *Night Vale*'s poem-like passages hold the audience in a state of tension between a presumed meaning and an intended one.

While these cold opens frequently target pop culture (Cecil perverts the theme song to *The Facts of Life* in "Orange Grove" [episode 38] and *Forrest Gump*'s "life is like a box of chocolates" quote in "A Beautiful Dream" [episode 34]), they make a more definite nod to their poetic roots in "Numbers" (episode 42). Here, Cecil offers a small homage, riffing on Walt Whitman: "I sing the body electric. I gasp the body organic. I miss the body remembered." If we accept Auden's "poetry as memorable speech" as our Occam's razor, then these openings—compact, rhythmic, quotable—make their own case as a form of *Night Vale*'s own, especially rooted in their omnipresent turns and the tension these create.

Poetry returns at the close of each *Night Vale* episode as well. In his haunting cadence, Cecil ushers the audience back into the world of mundanity and reason: "Good / night // Night / Vale, // Good night." These six syllables are pregnant with pauses and, like the openings, are lineated here in order to reflect the length and intensity. Each small silence measures itself against the others, verbal speed bumps that imbue this closing with an unsettling, even sinister, quality. Their languid, exacting pronunciation is too practiced to be anything but poetic, bookending each episode with the same invigoration of language as the opening.

These pauses, deliberate as they are, create and modulate the tension that is so vital for making *Night Vale* weird, unique, unsettling—even creepy at times. The uncertainty inherent in these pauses allows for these phrases, these "lines," to be interpreted in new and exciting combinations. Although the breath in "night // Night" is strong, the two words can still be read together, not just separately, making something like a dark lullaby. Stretching the space between words suspends them like individual beads on a necklace—they may contribute to a whole, but they also have other identities, both singularly and in relation to one another.

In his introduction in *Mostly Void* to the transcript for *Night Vale*'s freshman episode, "Pilot," Fink is surprised to find so many of the show's core features and storylines already present—including Old Woman Josie and the forbidden Dog Park. In terms of craft, "Pilot" also exemplifies the intrusive poetry that *Night Vale* would use throughout its run as both a vessel for and an antidote to capitalism and the banality of advertising. This ode to the lights above the Arby's was, in fact, the first piece of *Night Vale* to be written at all, the core around which the rest of the episode and the podcast itself crystallized. Transcribed according to its sounds and pauses, we might read it as:

> Lights, // seen in the sky above the Arby's. // Not / the glowing sign / of Arby's. // Something higher / and beyond that. // We know the difference. // We've caught on to their game. // We understand / the lights above Arby's / game. // Invaders / from another world. // Ladies and gentlemen / the future / is here. // And it's about a hundred feet / above / the Arby's.

Each pause is practiced and deliberate, creating both space and tension. The audience is forced to wait within these microseconds of silence, held in suspense—and *suspended* in a moment. Even the smallest pauses can introduce a powerful ambiguity, an uncertainty about how these words will fit together.

It's certainly not an isolated incident. Advertising in *Night Vale* leads to some of the podcast's most disjointed leaps of logic, offering only the most oblique connections to the products being advertised, if any at all. In "Glow Cloud" (episode 2), a message from Coca-Cola comes in the form of a disjointed wordscape: "I took a walk on the cool sand dunes, brittle grass overgrown, and above me, in the night sky, above me, I saw." Fragmented, circuitous, lush, saturated with image: If one of *Welcome to Night Vale*'s stated goals is to make the mundane into the strange, what better subversion could there be than transforming the anodyne landscape of advertising into art in general and poetry in specific?

In the first episode of the two-parter "The Sandstorm" (episode 19A), Home Depot's ad blares with refrains and repetitions: "Need help? Incomplete? Having feelings? Strange feelings? Feelings you've never felt? Incomplete?" These phrases repeat time and again, sometimes verbatim and other times mutated. When we return for the second part of "The Sandstorm," the ad is different—now for StrexCorp, a monolithic and sinister company that serves as the antagonist for Night Vale's first major story arc: "Got something to say? Need to say it? Unfulfilled? Never made sense of who you are? What you are? What you will be? Unfulfilled?" In their mirrored content and use of refrain, both halves of this ad create their own miniature form with its own rules on structure.

These intrusions apply only to those brands and industries that come from our own world. The local businesses of Night Vale, from Dark Owl Records to the Desert Flower Bowling Alley and Arcade Fun Complex, seem to be largely exempt. That's no real surprise, given that these flights of poetic fancy disarm the overwhelming reality of the audience's experiences with the everyday brands that populate every city in America. Night Vale and its businesses are already weird enough. The only notable exception is StrexCorp—and like our own mundane brands, the "weirding" of their advertising may reflect that we as an audience need to understand that StrexCorp is odd and uncanny, even within the logic of Night Vale.

A similar tactic is employed in "Subway" (episode 29), although the advertisement does not address any specific brand or company. In a segment purportedly about the financial markets, Cecil instead slips into a second-person torrent of image, though it is less staccato than other examples. It is more like the even flatness that many perceive as stereotypical of a bookstore poetry reading: "You will turn yourself / inside out. // Your sadness / will know / no bounds. // Ladybugs / will flee you; // wolves / run wild in you. // You will hear the wind chimes / like shattering. // The sun / will drip / ichor."

We can see other examples of poetic intrusion—in its most literal form—during "The Woman from Italy" (episode 39). Throughout this episode, Cecil frequently breaks out into a nasally sing-song voice; at each of these interruptions, the narrative is brushed aside and replaced by paired quatrains describing the titular Woman from Italy as a Baba Yaga-esque bogeyman. Once completed, these interludes of limerick horror recede, and the audience rejoins Cecil as if nothing had happened. Four of these interruptions occur throughout the episode, and all are markedly strange— the woman is apparently immortal and apocalyptic, "the end of all things," a juggernaut who skins her victims. They are not, however, true *non sequiturs*, as each happens while Cecil is reporting (although he does not seem to understand why) on the minutiae of a new visitor to town as she window-shops or drinks a cup of coffee. Strangest of all, though, is the way in which these brief poems also become meta-elements of the episode, co-opting Cecil's usual way of segueing between sections: "It's your skin that she wants, / bound and browned into leather // But first, pre-decease, / I give you the weather." The last ode to the Woman from Italy's recent carnage includes Cecil's closing "Good night," suggesting that these interruptions are more like momentary possessions, showing Cecil in the Woman's grips as if she were some cataclysmic muse.

At times, *Night Vale* even foregrounds its own relation to poetry. In "Poetry Week" (episode 20), the podcast features poems submitted by Twitter followers, with Cecil dutifully reporting on them as in-universe texts devised during the titular Poetry Week. These examples showcase considerable diversity: long-lined and doggedly short, ornately worded and ferociously stark. No poem in "Poetry Week" is simply a poem, either—they serve as propaganda, legislation, and even an unwise invitation to the forbidden Dog Park, which leads to the (temporary) disappearance of then-intern Dana.

The most telling of the poems, however, comes in the form of a sheet of paper from the head of the Night Vale Tourism board. Three human teeth are taped to the missive, which reads simply: "TOURISM IS IMPORTANT." Cecil's immediate reaction is to dismiss it, saying, "I thought, this is not poetry. This is visual art, but that's mere semantics." This hits close to discussions that have surrounded countless liminal poets and poems; Dickinson's "envelope poems" are sometimes regarded as inseparable from the literal envelopes on which they were originally written (Lerner). A knee-jerk reaction to disregard poetry that seems wildly heterodox or experimental is certainly not unique to Cecil either. When Aram Saroyan published a one-word poem—"lighght"—it enflamed a longstanding debate about what, exactly, poetry was (Daly).

In Saroyan's case, his poem was published in an American National Endowment for the Arts-funded collection, provoking exhausting refrains about wasteful government spending and the self-indulgence of pretentious artists. But in *Night Vale*, we see that same ancient debate instantly resolve, at least for Cecil—his definition of poetry expands to encompass multitudes. By resisting his instincts about what poetry is, Cecil signals an uncertainty and inclusivity that is essential to modern poetics. Yes, poetry can be ragged lines and careful versification, but it can also be something unexpected, something to be experienced more than understood. To any audience with a measure of sensitivity or context, "[i]nability to define ... does not preclude ability to differentiate" (Clements and Dunham 5). In 1964, Justice Stewart of the Supreme Court famously said of pornography, "I shall not today attempt to further define the kinds of material I understand to be embraced within that shorthand; and perhaps I could never succeed in intelligibly doing so. But I know it when I see it." Like obscenity, poetry may be best defined and identified only through contrast and resemblance: We know it when we see it, or in the case of *Night Vale*, when we hear it.

Existing somewhere between prose and verse, between performance and text, *Welcome to Night Vale* might also be understood through the lens of prose poetry, itself a system of symbolic tension, a seemingly paradoxical construct that exists between—and threatens the boundaries of—the genres that birthed it. Deprived of poetry's oldest tools in versification and lineation, the prose poet's greatest challenge, as Clements and Dunham emphasize, is "to find another way to generate tension within the poem ... via surrealistic anti-logic, bizarre narrative, lushness of language, innovative structure, or experiments with grammar and syntax" (4).

All of these struggles and strategies translate well to *Night Vale*, albeit in aural rather than written form. The genre of prose poetry is enriched by what Murphy calls "the infinitely extensive paragraph—with its capacity to drag the reader along the syncopated stream of the poet's rambling thoughts" (47–48). Here, of course, it is not that paragraph that may be "infinitely extensible," but the monologue. That flexibility—a fine reminder that the paragraph and its spoken equivalent are more units of meaning than of length—deepens the audience's uncertainty about what will come next and what form it might eventually take.

All of these poetic constructions and qualities imbue *Welcome to Night Vale* with unfamiliar vigor and clarity, giving a framework for its stated aim to render that which we know and expect as alien and novel. The strategies that undergird poetry help to empower the podcast, interrupting the smooth flow of narrative by refocusing the audience's attention to the language itself; this attention is destabilizing and sensuous all at once, so that same language becomes increasingly ephemeral, widening the gap between signifier and signified. *Night Vale* makes everything strange—and what better and more familiar target could they have than their own language? It falls apart, gently and often beautifully.

Beyond foregrounding the podcast's most valuable tool in making its language reflect the surrealism inherent to its content, reading *Night Vale* through the lens of poetry can provide a model for how poetry can interact with and energize modern media. The Cassandras of literature have bemoaned the death of poetry since its very inception—but our new genres are built from the bones (and still-living flesh) of those that came before, and to understand one enhances our appreciation of the other.

Poetry also helps to situate *Night Vale* in an unstable social context; in his 2016 essay, "On the Hatred of Poetry," Ben Lerner argues that poetry's unique position in popular perception comes from "the sense of poetry's tremendous stakes (combined with a sense of its tremendous social marginalization)" (13). As a society, we are often uncertain of poetry's place because it is surrounded by prestige, mystique, and suspicion—its history as a "high art" makes it inaccessible, or at least causes many people who might otherwise find some delight in it to regard it as an inaccessible cipher of pretensions and allusions. At the same time, it is taken as gospel by many that only poets still read poetry, leaving it as an exploded and impotent form despite its (at least theoretical) cultural cache.

Night Vale occupies a similar liminal space, the intersection between high and low culture, between the new and the familiar. We might call this particular overlap "highbrow geekery," a subset of popular culture that resists common perceptions about the lowest common denominator. It's accessible, both in the sense of its literal availability online and its ability to attract listeners, but it's also dense, provocative, and artful in its themes and construction. We sense that there is something at stake in identifying with Night Vale and its casually deranged inhabitants; perhaps our own identity as weird, as outré, as liminals ourselves? It's a feeling that poets and lovers of poetry have grappled with continuously, and foregrounding *Welcome to Night Vale*'s poem-like qualities draws attention to some common suspicions that surround any attempt to make language unambiguously weird—or at least to show that language is and has always *been* unambiguously weird.

Language, perhaps the defining feature of human intelligence and the bright line most draw between ourselves and the animal world, is an imperfect tool. In the late satirist, humorist, and humanist Terry Pratchett's *Death and What Comes Next*, the personification of Death (who speaks entirely in capital letters) offers up this response to an intransigent philosopher, saying that humanity was "TRYING TO UNDERSTAND THE COMPLEXITIES OF CREATION VIA A LANGUAGE THAT EVOLVED IN ORDER TO TELL ONE ANOTHER WHERE THE RIPE FRUIT WAS" (254). This isn't an insult, though—merely an observation that as humans, we have done wondrous, transcendent, and heartbreaking things with a tool whose sensitivity and meaning are pale reflections of the reality we perceive. Poetry, *Welcome to Night Vale*, and anything else that draws our attention to the crudeness of language unsettles us because language is so central to our humanity and our perception of the world around us. Language crumbles under the weight of our attention, like a single word repeated until it loses meaning. The things that imbue language with its greatest pleasures also do the most to destroy the illusion of our certainty about the world we inhabit. That tension is a precious thing; in refreshing it, *Welcome to Night Vale* proves its poetic prowess, offering us the chance to see our world anew, in all its beautiful, comical, terrifying strangeness.

WORKS CITED

Clements, Bryan, and Jamey Dunham. *An Introduction to the Prose Poem.* Firewheel Editions, 2009.

Daly, Ian. "You Call That Poetry?" *Poetry Foundation.* Accessed February 15, 2017. https://www.poetryfoundation.org/features/articles/detail/68913.

Fink, Joseph, and Jeffrey Cranor. *The Great Glowing Coils of the Universe.* Harper Perennial, 2016a.

———. *Mostly Void, Partially Stars.* Harper Perennial, 2016b.

Firchow, Peter. *W. H. Auden: Contexts for Poetry.* University of Delaware Press, 2002.

Jacobellis v. Ohio. U.S. Supreme Court. June 22, 1964.

Lerner, Ben. *The Hatred of Poetry.* Farrar, Straus and Giroux, 2016.

Murphy, Margueritte. *A Tradition of Subversion: The Prose Poem in English from Wilde to Ashbury.* The University of Massachusetts Press, 1992.

Orr, David. *Beautiful & Pointless: A Guide to Modern Poetry.* Harper Perennial, 2012.

Pratchett, Terry. "Death and What Comes Next." In *A Blink of the Screen,* ed. Terry Pratchett, 252–254. Doubleday, 2012.

"Rita Dove." Lannan. Accessed February 15, 2017. http://www.lannan.org/bios/rita-dove.

Shelley, Percy Bysshe. "A Defense of Poetry." In *A Defense of Poetry and Other Essays.* Project Gutenberg, 2004. Accessed February 15, 2017. http://www.gutenberg.org/files/5428/5428-h/5428-h.htm.

Wheeler, Lesley. *Voicing American Poetry: Sound and Performance from the 1920s to the Present.* Cornell University Press, 2008.

Yakich, Mark. "What Is a Poem?" *The Atlantic,* November 25, 2013. Accessed February 15, 2017. https://www.theatlantic.com/entertainment/archive/2013/11/what-is-a-poem/281835/.

"Fear the Night Sky!": On the Nightvalian Void and an Ethics of Risk

Line Henriksen

Abstract Staring up at the night sky, the host of Night Vale's community radio wonders about the void behind the stars, "that nothingness that is everything, that everything that is nothing," as he calls it. This chapter explores the Nightvalian void, which seems to be omnipresent yet indifferent to the humans observing it. It does so by drawing connections to a western cultural and historical imaginary in which tele-technologies—such as radio—were considered to be mediated by the void of the so-called etheric ocean. This void-like ocean was a medium for conquest and exploration, but also a source of anxiety, for, as Cecil puts it, "what if the void is not as *void* as we thought? What could be coming towards us out of the distance?" There is no simple answer to Cecil's questions since the void cannot be fully known nor understood. Instead, *Welcome to Night Vale* seems to suggest that living in the presence of such uncertainty is unavoidable. Exploring the imaginaries of the Nightvalian void, this chapter argues that the podcast does not soothe the anxieties sparked by the void, but instead explores ways to stay with the constant threat—and promise—of the arrival of *something* out of *nothing*.

L. Henriksen (✉)
Centre for Gender Studies, University of Copenhagen, Copenhagen, Denmark
e-mail: vwx210@hum.ku.dk

© The Author(s) 2018
J. A. Weinstock (ed.), *Critical Approaches to* Welcome to Night Vale,
https://doi.org/10.1007/978-3-319-93091-6_9

Keywords Void • Ethics • Radio • Telecommunication • Time • Space

"Here's a public service message to all the children in our audience," radio host Cecil Palmer declares, continuing:

> Children, the night sky may seem like a scary thing sometimes. And it is. It's a very scary thing. Look at the stars, twinkling silently. They are so far away that none of us will ever get to even the closest one. They are dead-eyed sigils of our own failures against distance and mortality. And behind them, just the void. That nothingness that is everything, that everything that is nothing. Even the blinking light of an airplane streaking across it does not seem to assuage the tiniest bit of its blackness, like throwing a single stray ember into the depths of a vast arctic ocean. And what if the void is not as void as we thought? What could be coming towards us out of the distance? Insentient asteroid with a chance trajectory? Sentient beings with a malicious trajectory? What good could come of this? What good, children, could come of *any* of this? Fear the night sky, children. And sleep tight in your beds, and the inadequate shelters of blankets and parental love. Sleep sound, children.
>
> This has been our Children's Fun Fact Science Corner. (Episode 24, "The Mayor"; Fink and Cranor, *Mostly Void* 240)

To the small town of Night Vale, the void is omnipresent. Whether it takes the shape of the desert surrounding the town, the depth of outer space or even a puddle on the floor,[1] the nothingness of the void is inescapable. Indeed, according to Cecil, this nothingness is everything, and this everything is nothing. But why does the void feature so prominently in the stories of *Welcome to Night Vale*? Why is nothingness materialized as one of the more terrifying monsters of Night Vale? And what, indeed, may be coming toward us from the distance? Exploring the historical interconnections between the figure of the void and wireless technology, I suggest that the void may be understood as an expression of existential groundlessness in increasingly digitalized societies as well as in a world in perceived crisis. It may also, however, present something different: a horizon of the unknown and the possibility of the impossible as *something* arrives from out of *nothing*. In this sense, perhaps Cecil's rhetorical question—what good could come of this?—is a deeply ethical one, relating to the larger issue of how one greets the arrival of the unknown. What good, children, can come of thinking ethics through the void?

Voices from the Void

While describing the void in the Children's Fun Fact Science Corner, Cecil likens it to a cold, arctic ocean that swallows the light and warmth of an ember. The void, he says, is a constant reminder of human failure in the face of distance and mortality. It is not, however, only the void that reminds Cecil of distances; it is also the medium of radio itself: "it is possible that I am alone in an empty universe, speaking to no one, unaware that the world is held aloft merely by my delusions and my smooth, sonorous voice," he says in another broadcast. "More on this story as it develops, I say, possibly only to myself" ("The Shape in Grove Park," episode 5; Fink and Cranor, *Mostly Void* 43).

The medium of radio—and by extension podcast—makes it possible to communicate across vast distances, but in so doing it may also, paradoxically, remind its listeners of these distances, enforcing a sense of loneliness, isolation, and even helplessness. As Cecil puts it, when witnessing what he thinks is the death of Carlos, the man he loves, "here I am, stuck in my booth, useless, only able to narrate, not to help" ("One Year Later," episode 25; *Mostly Void* 252).

The interconnections between voids, distances, isolation, (icy) oceans, and wireless technology have a long history that reaches back to the early days of radio. Media theorist Jeffrey Sconce explains that radio undid the otherwise grounded experience of wired connections and unleashed an invisible, omnipresent wandering signal on the world. There was a sense of wonder, freedom, and adventure associated with this wandering signal, but also increasingly a sense of anxiety. Wireless technology undid time and space by making the distant near and the near distant, and it troubled the concept of "presence," since something could be heard and felt, yet without being there in the flesh. Wireless signals seemed to envelop people's bodies without their knowledge and without them being able to see it. Some, such as radio enthusiasts who fished the ether for "voices from the void" (Sconce 64), welcomed this ghostly touch.[2] For them, connection became more important than communication and meaning. For others, however, such enveloping presented the risk of becoming "lost at sea," which "implied that, as with the oceans of the earth, unknown creatures might stalk this electronic sea's invisible depths" (Sconce 69).

Nautical metaphors were used in order to describe and imagine the ghostly omnipresent absence of wireless, and the "etheric ocean" became the primary structuring metaphor (Sconce 63). The metaphor may have been born from the nautical roots of wireless technology—it was created for ships to communicate with one another as well as with land while sailing the voids of the world's oceans—and the technology's ability to envelop and subsume, like an ocean. It also indicated how the developments in technology both mirrored and aided socio-political disturbances and changes of the time. The "etheric ocean" became a structuring metaphor for the experience of suspension in an invisible ocean caused as much by ghostly signals as what Sconce refers to as a perceived loss of the "moral and cultural grounding" of the West (64). Rapid societal changes meant that the metaphor of being "lost at sea" captured a sense of constant movement, disturbance and the suspension above an abyss full of possible monsters. Something was coming from out of the depth and the distance, but what?

On the night of April 15, 1912, the anxiety-inducing interconnections between oceans and wireless became more pronounced as the *Titanic* hit an iceberg. Due to technological difficulties and missed connections, only one ship responded to the *Titanic*'s call for help. In the wake of the tragedy, wireless technology therefore became associated both with something benign and useful as well as something disturbing, considering how wireless technology worked to broadcast the news of the tragedy while unable—or unwilling?—to interfere. According to Sconce, the *Titanic* thus "forever imprint[ed] on the mind's eye the image of unfortunate souls spread across the icy void of the Atlantic, struggling to stay above the surface. Above this tragic scene, in turn, hovered the eerie ocean of wireless, which had provided the agonizingly immediate account of the catastrophe even as it powerfully reiterated the gulf separating sender and receiver, victim and savior" (74). As Cecil would go on to say in 2013: "here I am, stuck in my booth, useless, only able to narrate, not to help" (episode 25, "One Year Later").

The etheric ocean was, according to Sconce, eventually reined in, and radio became a medium of scheduled broadcasts rather than a strange void to be fished for voices. Subsequent technologies, such as TV, follow much the same format, yet with the arrival of the internet, the nautical metaphors returned, turning the world wide web into a sea of *phishing*, *surfing*, *streaming*, and *piracy*, as well as a place of surface and depth, considering how its unindexed parts are referred to as the Deep Web. In the Deep Web one does have to fish for information from a fluid and flowing etheric ocean, but with caution, since this is a place rumored to be the home of monsters, both human and—according to internet lore—supernatural. Hackers, pedophiles, and pushers rub shoulders with AIs and spectral monsters that all threaten to swallow up any hapless traveler caught in the waves of the web. A Google image search will show that this web sea with all its dangerous depths is typically visualized as an iceberg portraying the layers of the cold, arctic ocean of the web, warning you that the deeper you go, the more dangerous it gets.[3]

I suggest that a legacy of the etheric ocean can be found in the oceanic metaphors and monsters that structure and inhabit the world wide web. This legacy may also be what rears its head in Cecil's broadcasts in the shape of the void as an anxiety-inducing, indifferent horizon of both connection and distance, community and isolation. It is deep and cold, an arctic ocean that may or may not harbor unknown creatures that are currently heading toward the podcast listeners from out of the distance. Indeed, just by moving through a digitalized society, the podcast listener bathes in an etheric ocean of waves and ghostly signals,[4] not unlike those who tried to steer the first etheric ocean. But is the omnipresence of the void in *Welcome to Night Vale* merely a question of a lingering metaphor from modernity? Or is there more to the re-emergence of the void as a contemporary monster and monster-filled space?

IN FREE FALL

Suggesting a thought experiment, media theorist Hito Steyerl asks you to "[i]magine you are falling. But there is no ground" (1). Without a ground, one seems to be tumbling not toward certain death but through an abyssal void. Yet, one may not experience it as such, Steyerl argues, considering how "[f]alling is relational—if there is nothing to fall toward, you may not even be aware that you are falling … it may actually feel like perfect stasis—as if history and time have ended and you can't even remember that time ever moved forward." According to Steyerl, the experience of groundlessness and stasis due to falling is something that can be attributed to the present moment, when we—a broadly defined western "we"— "cannot assume any stable ground on which to base metaphysical claims or foundational political myths" (1).

Steyerl's free fall is reminiscent of Sconce's abyssal void of wireless. As previously mentioned, Sconce argues that the void of the etheric ocean and the anxiety it induced was related to—both mirroring and exacerbating—socio-political disturbances and rapid changes. The experience of moral and cultural groundlessness and lack of foundation found its perfect image in the abyssal void of contemporary advanced tele-technology and its ability to provide contact (or lack thereof) over meaning. Something similar seems to be at stake in Night Vale, where meaning and common sense and common ground are constantly renegotiated. As the Faceless Old Woman Who Secretly Lives in Your Home puts it, voicing a concern not dissimilar to Cecil's when he wondered whether his smooth, sonorous voice is all that keeps the world together:

> [Y]our words hold a lot of meaning intrinsically. Almost everything we say does. If you looked at any word in the English language close enough, you would see within the great, glowing coils of the universe unwinding ... Our language holds the key to it. The key to the unraveling of all things. I think that one day this world will simply talk itself to death and I will be left to flit about in the void. I will be the Faceless Old Woman Who Secretly Lives Nowhere. ("Condos," unnumbered live show; Fink and Cranor, *Mostly Void* 266)

As argued by Steyerl, the free fall brings about a sense of the dissolution of history and time, and in the Faceless Old Woman's tale the unraveling of meaning creates a Nowhere, the "empty universe," perhaps, mentioned by Cecil—a groundless void. This unraveling of history and time is constantly at play in Night Vale to a point where the scientist and outsider/interloper Carlos is surprised to learn that time does not work in the small desert town: "Cecil, sorry to bother you," he says. "I need you to get the word out that clocks in Night Vale are not real. I have not found a single real clock. I have disassembled several watches and clocks this week and all of them are hollow inside. No gears, no crystal, no battery or power source. Some of them actually contain a gelatinous grey lump that seems to be growing hair and teeth" ("The Phone Call," episode 16; *Mostly Void* 147). It is strangely fitting that time in Night Vale has teeth; rather than work linearly, time swallows and envelops, plummeting Carlos into a free fall. As Cecil reports in another episode:

> Carlos and his scientists at the monitoring station near Route 800 say their seismic monitors have been indicating wild seismic shifts, meaning to say that the ground should be going up and down all over the place. I don't know about you, folks, but the ground has been as still as the crust of a tiny globe rocketing through an endless void could be. Carlos says that they've double-checked the monitors, and they are in perfect working order. To put it plainly, there appears to be catastrophic earthquakes happening right here in Night Vale that absolutely no one can feel. ("Pilot," episode 1; *Mostly Void* 7)

Carlos' instruments, on which he relied in order to assign a specific and unmoving meaning to the strange depths that are Night *Vale*, merely send him into a free fall through the endless void that surrounds the tiny globe on which he lives—a globe that, according to the Faceless Old Woman, may soon dissolve as well.

In *Welcome to Night Vale*, meaning threatens to unravel, undoing any sense of foundational truth—whether of science or language—and plunging people into the abyss, making the void not just a harborer of monsters, but a boundless, hungry monster in its own right. I suggest that this may echo the legacy of wireless technology imagined as an etheric ocean, as well as a sense of socio-political lack of grounding, which can also be detected in other digital narratives such as, for example, Chuck Tingle's "Tingleverse."

Cosmic Horror in Times of Crisis

"[N]ice try but buckaroos know the rules of The Void up top is PRESIDENT BANNON and bottom is crying DEVILBOY TROMP this is way of cosmic horor,"[5] tweets erotica author Tingle[6] in a response to a tweet by American President Donald Trump, and: "WOW YOU ARE SO LOUD IN THE VOID YOUR CRABS MUST BE SQUEALING."[7] According to Tingle, the world is called the Tingleverse, and it "has a top and bottom but is infinate in between. top is this layer, bottom is The Tingularity. Outside these layers is The Void."[8] It is from The Void that monsters sometimes enter what he refers to as "this timeline" (there are infinite timelines in the Tingleverse), one of them being the Devilman Tromp, who is a skinsuit filled with void crabs.

In the speculative and humorous worlds of Tingle, The Void is a disturbing, sea-like horizon from which monsters emerge, echoing Cecil's worried question: "And what if the void is not as void as we thought? What could be coming towards us out of the distance?" With its tentacle monsters and cosmic horrors (or to be exact "cosmic *horor*"), the Tingleverse seems inspired by the work of H. P. Lovecraft, as is *Welcome to Night Vale* itself.[9] Indeed, the twenty-first century has seen an increased academic and artistic interest in the works of Lovecraft, in which existential terror in the encounter with unknowable, indifferent and boundless forces of the universe plays an immense role. In the collection *The Age of Lovecraft*, Carl H. Sederholm and Jeffrey Andrew Weinstock describe Lovecraft's work as an undoing of perceived human exceptionalism, explaining that Lovecraft's work reminds its readers that "however grand we consider human accomplishment, it will all inevitably disappear into the unplumbable depths of deep time." Like Carlos' fanged clocks, Lovecraftian time swallows and undoes rather than run according to the linear trajectory fashioned by a human concept of—to reference Steyerl—history and time.

Like the void of the etheric ocean, Lovecraft's cosmic void of deep time has returned to haunt the twenty-first century with a legacy of socio-political disruption, uncertainty, and a thorough undoing of perceived human mastery and exceptionalism. This resurfacing may have to do with the experience of crisis that seems to haunt present-day western societies. With the financial crisis, the so-called refugee crisis, the specter of terrorism, the UK withdrawing from the EU, rising nationalism and populism, and global warming, any attempt at founding a common ground seems to be constantly undone. In such times, the internet—the offspring of the etheric ocean—appears to magnify the workings of this groundlessness as it has become associated with "fake news" and "post-truth," as well as leaked information and lack of accountability. The stories by Tingle are an example of the popularity of the figure of the void in current internet-storytelling, as is *Welcome to Night Vale*. In both worlds—the Tingleverse and Night Vale—the void becomes a way of expressing a sense of anxiety and fear in the face of disruptive changes that seem indifferent to the suffering of human beings. In the void, there is no moral ground, nor any common ground—but perhaps there is something else?

A Risky Ethics of the Void

In Night Vale, as in the Tingleverse,[10] words tend toward the surreal, which undermines common sense and even common ground, for what is everyday life in Night Vale is strange to the listeners of the podcast *Welcome to Night Vale* and vice versa. Looking at the context in which *Welcome to Night Vale* is created as well as the medium through which it is broadcast, the performance of the nonsensical and lack of grounding may reflect and actively engage with a broader experience of groundlessness in times of (perceived) crisis. This is also what makes the void a horizon of impossibility, and—I will argue—the beginning not of morality but of what poststructuralist, feminist philosopher Margrit Shildrick calls an "ethics of risk" (3). She explains:

In place of a morality of principles and rules that speaks to a clear-cut set of binaries setting out the good and the evil, the self and the other, normal and abnormal, the permissible and the prohibited, I turn away from such normative ethics to embrace instead the ambiguity and unpredictability of an openness towards the monstrous other. It is a move that acknowledges both vulnerability to the other, and the vulnerability of the self. The question of value here is not so much made irrelevant, as disrupted, suspended in the face of an encounter that cannot be known in advance. (3)

The encounter with the unexpected other disrupts and suspends the question of value, suggesting a sense of depth and loss of ground. Whereas morality needs a stable foundation in order to separate good from bad, an ethics of risk is relational, like the free fall itself, and turned toward that which is yet to come, expecting the unexpected. The risk lies in its demand that you stay open to encountering the unexpected, and how this openness will disturb the very threshold between self and other, inside and outside, changing any sense of a stable identity.

It is in the openness toward the unexpected and unpredictable—that which is arriving from out of the void—that new and different foundations become possible. As Steyerl puts it, "falling does not only mean falling apart, it can also mean a new certainty falling into place. Grappling with crumbling futures that propel us backwards onto an agonizing present, we may realize that the place we are falling toward is no longer grounded, nor is it stable. It promises no community, but a shifting formation" (9). In the undoing of space and time that takes place in the free fall, something different becomes possible, a new perspective, perhaps, or maybe even a home. Back in Night Vale, Carlos is aware of this. After having attempted to ground himself and Cecil in a condo described as "perfect," he is almost drawn directly into the ground and buried there. Instead of perfection and being grounded so well and deep that he may never be able to get out again, he turns to nothingness to sketch out a home:

I was thinking about the series of ongoing actions that we perceive as the present. And the amassing of memories that we treat as the living record of the past. And the hopes and dreams and assumptions that we project as the future. I was thinking about time and about how it means something to so many people and about how it's so finite and also so infinite.

I was also thinking about space, about how it is nothing. And then a point, which is just a single spot within the nothing, and a line which separates the nothing into two nothings. And how a plane is a patch of nothing, and an angle just where two nothings meet. But all of those things combined, an object of points, lines, planes, and angles. An object with length and width and depth that can take up actual space. How that object becomes something made of nothing, within nothing. An object can be a wall, a floor, a roof, a bed, a table, a dog, a door, a rug, a … a home. ("Condos," unnumbered live show; Fink and Cranor, *Mostly Void* 277)

Carlos imagines *nothing* turning into *something*, which offers a slightly different perspective to Cecil's fearful "this nothing that is everything, this everything that is nothing." Nothingness, in taking away stable foundations, can make room for something different, such as the home of a same-sex couple, which is still not a part of the normative foundations of any current western society.

In a world in free fall, different lines of dis/orientation can be drawn, and new navigational tools found, creating different, but never static, foundations.[11] In the undoing of space and time that takes place in the free fall, something different becomes possible, a new perspective perhaps, as one looks into the abyssal void no longer sure what is up and what is down, what is left and what is right—or even what is self and what is other.

An Overview

There is no stable foundation in the void, and it is by welcoming this instability, the fluidity of the etheric ocean, that something different may take form—if only for a while—before changing again. What good could come of this? Cecil asked, and it is likely that what is closing in from the distance is nothing good at all. It does, however, embody a hope that the impossible may yet be possible and that disruptions and transformation can be pushed in directions that make marginalized lives more livable.[12] In times of crisis and suspension in a digital, etheric ocean where foundations are made and unmade with the click of a mouse, the void becomes a monstrous figure of fear, but also one of different perspectives and an im/possible ethics of risk. It promises different lives, different loves and, perhaps, a different home that will ground you for a while before a new encounter sends you falling again—into nothingness.

And now back to our host, Cecil:

Well listeners, this has been another day, another night, another bit of time in this bit of space. I'm sitting at my desk, feet planted on old, thinning carpet, but in my mind I am anywhere but. I am above, in the sky above, looking down at our little Night Vale. I see the lights, in grids and curves, and the places where there are no lights, because they are off or missing or invisible. I see roads with cars, and the cars have people in them, and the people are traveling through the dark in the comfort and light of the cars, and I see all of this from above. I see where the town gives way gradually to the desert, the last few lights from the last few homesteads, like stray sparks from a campfire, tossed out into the absolute black of the scrublands and the sand wastes. I see the orbit of citizen around citizen, all these ordinary Night Valians, about their ordinary lives in this singular, extraordinary place we call home ... And, looking up, I see only the stars and the void, all a little closer than they were before. All still so unreachably distant. ("The Traveler," episode 18; *Mostly Void* 168)

Notes

1. "There's still an empty OJ glass on the floor. The carpet around it is dark, not with liquid stain but with void" ("Orange Grove," episode 38; *Great Glowing* 134–35).
2. For more on the ability of wireless to "touch," see Lisa Blackman's work on the concept of "mental touch."
3. Based on a Google image search on February 15, 2017.
4. See, for example, the "Digital Ethereal" project, which makes visible the rainbow-colored ghosts of wireless signals that are usually invisible to the human eye. http://www.digitalethereal.com/. Accessed February 15, 2017.
5. Chuck Tingle (@ChuckTingle) on Twitter, February 6, 2017. https://twitter.com/ChuckTingle/status/828660349758959617. Accessed February 15, 2017. All misspellings should be assumed to be present in the original.
6. "Chuck Tingle" is a pseudonym and a persona.
7. Chuck Tingle (@ChuckTingle) on Twitter, February 10, 2017. https://twitter.com/ChuckTingle/status/829847028620353536. Accessed February 15, 2017.
8. Chuck Tingle (@ChuckTingle) on Twitter, January 29, 2017. https://twitter.com/ChuckTingle/status/825484077759213568. Accessed February 15, 2017.

9. One of the creators of *Welcome to Night Vale*, Joseph Fink, has also edited the anthology *A Commonplace Book of the Weird—The Untold Stories of H.P. Lovecraft* (2010).

10. In the short essay "Dr. Chuck Tingle's Guide to Make Books Real," Tingle explains his writing style as well as struggles with writing.

11. Sara Ahmed's work on queer dis/orientation haunts these lines. She offers an important critique and discussion of which bodies get to survive in moments of disorientation, and which bodies that do not. I am unfortunately unable to go into detail with this discussion here, but it is important to keep in mind the power structures that make some bodies able to live in free fall whereas others perish. It is also important to keep in mind that the experience of free fall may not be anything new to people, who have lived their entire lives in the margin.

12. On livable lives, see Ahmed.

Works Cited

Ahmed, Sara. *Queer Phenomenology – Orientations, Objects, Others*. Duke University Press, 2006.

Blackman, Lisa. *Immaterial Bodies – Affect, Embodiment, Mediation*. Sage Publications, 2013.

Fink, Joseph, and Jeffrey Cranor. *The Great Glowing Coils of the Universe – Welcome to Night Vale Episodes, Volume 2*. Orbit, 2016a.

———. *Mostly Void, Partially Stars – Welcome to Night Vale Episodes, Volume 1*. Orbit, 2016b.

Sederholm, Carl H., and Jeffrey Andrew Weinstock. "Lovecraft Rising." In *The Age of Lovecraft*. Kindle edition, ed. Carl H. Sederholm and Jeffrey Andrew Weinstock, University of Minnesota Press, 2016.

Sconce, Jeffrey. *Haunted Media – Electronic Presence from Telegraphy to Television*. Duke University Press, 2000.

Shildrick, Margrit. *Embodying the Monster – Encounters with the Vulnerable Self*. Sage Publications, 2002.

Steyerl, Hito. "In Free Fall – A Thought Experiment on Vertical Perspective." *e-flux Journal* 24 (April 2011). Accessed March 9, 2017. http://www.e-flux.com/journal/24/67860/in-free-fall-a-thought-experiment-on-vertical-perspective/.

Tingle, Chuck. "Dr. Chuck Tingle's Guide to Make Books Real." *The Town Crier*, November 28, 2016. Accessed February 15, 2017. http://towncrier.puritan-magazine.com/ephemera/chuck-tingle/.

INDEX[1]

---

[1] Note: Page numbers followed by 'n' refer to notes.

© The Author(s) 2018
J. A. Weinstock (ed.), *Critical Approaches to* Welcome to Night Vale,
https://doi.org/10.1007/978-3-319-93091-6